Kiss Me, Stupid

"You know . . ." Joe whispered, his breath hot on her ears, "I'm still a bit frightened of you."

Lorna was moved. It hadn't occurred to her that he might be feeling as vulnerable as she was. She stood on tiptoe and whispered into his ear.

"You shouldn't be. Really. I don't bite."

"Honest? Do you promise not to set me an examination on how to be an ideal boyfriend?"

Lorna smiled confidently, but her heart was trembling. She couldn't believe that he was asking her to go out with him. She almost felt like crying.

"I promise."

Joe gazed into her eyes and smiled.

"So what do I do now?"

Lorna smiled back. There was only one thing they could do. She opened her mouth and, as she began to speak, wondered how far she was going to fall — knowing that, once their lips met, nothing would ever be the same again. She answered his question.

"Kiss me, stupid."

And he did.

D0259748

Also in the Point Romance series:

Point Romance

Kiss Me, Stupid

Alison Creaghan

Cover illustration by Derek Brazell

■SCHOLASTIC

Scholastic Children's Books,
Scholastic Publications Ltd,
7–9 Pratt Street, London NW1 0AE, UK

Scholastic Inc.,
555 Broadway, New York, NY 10012-3999, USA

Scholastic Canada Ltd,
123 Newkirk Road, Richmond Hill,
Ontario, Canada L4C 3G5

Ashton Scholastic Pty Ltd,
P O Box 579, Gosford, New South Wales,
Australia

Ashton Scholastic Ltd,
Private Bag 92801, Penrose, Auckland,
New Zealand

First published by Scholastic Publications Ltd, 1994

Text copyright © Alison Creaghan, 1994
Cover artwork copyright © Derek Brazell, 1994

ISBN 0 590 55520 0

Typeset by TW Typesetting, Midsomer Norton, Avon
Printed by Cox & Wyman Ltd, Reading, Berks.

10 9 8 7 6 5 4 3 2 1

Contents

Part 1

Chapter 1

When Lorna's alarm went off it was still dark. She reached over and, shivering, pressed the "snooze" button. Then she pulled the duvet more closely around her and tried to return to the pleasant dream she'd been having a moment before.

It didn't work. Just as she was slipping off again, Lorna heard the soft "plop" of mail coming through the letter box. Dimly, she remembered what day it was: Monday, February the fourteenth, Valentine's Day. Suppose. . . ?

Really, there was no "suppose" about it. Lorna knew that there wouldn't be a Valentine card waiting for her downstairs, any more than there had been on the fifteen other Valentine's Days since she was born. But now she was awake, and there was nothing for it but to get up.

While Lorna was in the bathroom, her alarm went off again. Its penetrating beep grew louder until it echoed through the house. Mum yelled from her bedroom.

"Turn that thing off, can't you? You'll wake up the whole neighbourhood!"

Lorna dried her face and headed back into her room, bumping into Ben, her thirteen-year-old brother, who was still in his pyjamas.

"Get out of my room!"

"I was just turning the alarm off," Ben complained.

Lorna slammed the door on Ben and started to get dressed. She was one of the few girls in her year who still wore the official school uniform: plain white blouse with black skirt or trousers. Today, Lorna put on black trousers, then a thick black jumper, concealing her modest figure. Then she spent five minutes brushing her long, blonde hair. Next, she put on a tiny dab of mascara and a faint trace of lipstick. For a moment, she looked like the sort of girl who boys sent Valentines to. But then she put on her round, metal framed glasses, making her face look more severe and academic. Time to pack her bag.

Today Lorna had English, Chemistry, Information Technology, Maths and Media Studies. She made sure that she had all the necessary books for each. Then she packed the novel that she was reading at the moment, *The Tenant of Wildfell Hall*, in case there was some time to read it during the day. She tended to get her work done more quickly than other people, and often had time left over at the end of lessons.

When she'd done up the straps on her bag, Lorna went downstairs. There were three letters on the mat in the hallway. She picked them up without looking at them and went into the kitchen. She filled the jug kettle, then, while she was waiting for it to boil, sliced some bread to make whole-meal toast. Most days she only had muesli, but today it was cold, and she felt like spoiling herself.

Mum came down just as Lorna was finishing her toast. Mum was still wearing her dressing gown and had bags under her eyes. This morning, she looked every day of her thirty-five years.

"There's plenty of tea in the pot," Lorna said to her. She couldn't quite bring herself to say "good morning", since Mum had shouted at her earlier. Mum grunted something in reply as she poured herself a mug. Then she went into the hall and yelled upstairs.

"Ben! You're going to be late! Get yourself down here!" Back in the kitchen, she asked,

"Any mail?"

Lorna pointed at it. Mum picked the three letters up and swore under her breath.

"Just what I need: a red reminder from the electricity." She paused. "Aah! I'd forgotten what day it was."

She held up an envelope.

"A card from Ric."

Lorna put on a smile. Ric was Mum's boyfriend, a lecturer at the Sixth Form college. He was five years younger than her. It didn't seem right, somehow, that Mum, in her mid-thirties, should have a young, handsome boyfriend, while Lorna, at sixteen, didn't. Mum opened the envelope. It contained a postcard of Rodin's statue, "The Kiss".

On the back of it, Ric had written "plenty more where this one came from, love, guess who?"

"Aah," Mum said again. "Isn't he a sweetie?"

Lorna said nothing. She liked Ric rather more than she would admit to her mother, but found it irritating, the way Mum went on about him.

"And who's this from?"

Mum held up the third envelope, then turned it round. "Recognize the writing?"

Lorna shook her head. How was she supposed to know the handwriting of Mum's anonymous admirers?

"Are you sure?"

Lorna frowned. There was a funny expression in Mum's eyes. Lorna looked at the envelope again. The address was printed in neat, anonymous letters. Instead of Ms K. Haines, it read Ms L. Haines. Lorna snatched it from her mother's hands.

"You didn't tell me you had a secret admirer," Mum teased. "Or didn't you know?"

"It's probably one of the girls at school, trying to be funny," Lorna snapped, blushing.

"Aren't you going to open it?"

"Later."

"Oh, come on, Lorna," Mum complained. "I showed you mine. Don't be a spoilsport."

"I'll show you later."

Before Mum could argue any more, Ben came in.

"Can't find a clean shirt."

"You're hopeless," Mum said. "You're going to be late, you realize that?"

"So am I," Lorna said, getting up. She put the card into the front zip-up section of her bag, next to her lunch box, and hurried out of the house.

Lorna walked to school the way she always did, with her shoulders straight and her head to the ground, defying anyone to get in her way. She could feel the presence of the Valentine card, ticking away loudly like a time-bomb concealed in her knapsack. Who was it from? Half of her believed what she'd told her mother, that it was one of her friends, having a joke. Only her friends weren't really like that.

As far as Lorna knew, she didn't have any enemies. There was no one who would tease her by sending a mock Valentine. Still, it was probably a joke. Except . . . there was just the possibility that the card was genuine. It was possible, Lorna had to admit to herself, that Mum was right. Somewhere, in this boring, provincial town, she had a secret admirer.

Lorna liked suspense. She liked TV serials with cliffhanger endings. She liked putting down books when she still had a chapter to go and waiting until the next day to find out the dark secret which, until now, had prevented the heroine from accepting the hero, or the real identity of the tall, dark stranger . . . Now the card in her bag gave her a delicious feeling of anticipation. Suppose, just suppose, that it was what she hoped? What kind of card would it be? Sensible or soppy? Romantic or silly?

Lorna got to the form room at twenty to nine,

ten minutes before registration. She was the first
girl to arrive. There were two boys in the room
already: James Matthews, a dull, hard-working
footballer, and Brian Kane, a long-haired, lanky
follower of obscure rock bands. Neither of them
acknowledged her. Lorna sat down in the far
corner of the room, by the window, beneath the
noticeboard, and got her card out. The writing
wasn't at all familiar, but it was definitely her
name. The postmark was local too, so it couldn't
be her dad playing a trick – an annoying thought
which had just occurred to her.

Lorna hoped that it would be a really romantic
card, like the one Ric had sent her mum. But she
was a realist. It was more likely to be a reminder
of her next dentist's appointment. Bracing herself for a disappointment, she sliced open the
envelope with her longest fingernail. Then, deli-
cately, she pulled the card out. Its white back
revealed no clues. She turned it round. This
wasn't a standard Valentine card. There was no
soppy message, only two silhouettes, one blue,
one white, dancing. She didn't know the picture,
but recognized the artist: Matisse. Whoever had
sent her this card had good taste. Slowly, she
opened it.

The message was printed in blue felt tip. Lorna
had to read it twice before she took in its meaning:

*One day, I'll work up the nerve to tell you how I
feel about you. Until then, this'll have to do.*

Beneath these two sentences was a large X.

"Hi!"

Lorna looked up. Her best friend, Sulvinder, was standing beside her.

"Let's have a look."

Lorna passed her the card. Sulvinder examined it with an amused glint in her eye.

"Who's it from?"

"I've no idea."

Sulvinder handed it back.

"I wouldn't show it to Abby, if I were you. She wouldn't believe you."

Lorna laughed.

"I know."

"It's nice though," Sulvinder said. "Can't be from anyone in this dump."

"I hope not," Lorna agreed, though she couldn't see how the sender could be from anywhere else. All the boys she knew went to Westtown Comp, and lived in Westtown itself, or the neighbouring village of Coddington. Lorna and Sulvinder agreed – all the boys at Westtown were a waste of time: immature, pathetic creatures who were always spoiling lessons by their silly behaviour. The two girls liked the idea of having boyfriends in theory, but not in practice – not if they were from the motley crew they'd spent the last five years at school with.

As Lorna put the card away, Abby arrived. She waved at Lorna and Sulvinder, then continued the conversation she was having with Lisa Strepton about Economics, a subject Lorna didn't do.

Abigail Thomas held similar views about boys

to Lorna's and Sulvinder's. She was academically ambitious and wasn't going to let anything or anyone interfere with her GCSEs. The only difference was that Abby, unlike the other two girls, was very glamorous-looking. She appeared much older than she actually was. Boys were always staring at Abby and developing major crushes on her. But few ever worked up the nerve to ask her out. If they did, Abby gave them very short shrift indeed.

A minute later, Abby came over to Lorna and Sulvinder's table.

"Look at these," she said, throwing a heap of Valentine cards onto the table. "Talk about lousy taste. *Yuck!*"

The girls examined the cards. There were six altogether. Two showed teddy bears, and had really soppy messages inside. Three contained risqué jokes of the "If I said you had a beautiful body would you hold it against me?" variety. The sixth pictured a helpless looking puppy, and was almost acceptable, in Lorna's eyes, if not Abby's. None was anywhere near as nice as the Matisse card.

"Do you know who they're from?" Sulvinder asked.

"Of course I do. Half of them are *signed*. This one's from James Black. This is from . . ." Abby listed the names with derision. Two of the senders were in their form, and in the room right now, but that didn't stop her. Lorna felt a little sorry for the helpless boys whose hearts Abby had captured. But only a little bit sorry. The senders must know

that they really had no chance with Abigail
Thomas. She said that she would date boys when
she was good and ready — and they wouldn't be
from Westtown Comprehensive.

Lorna handed the cards back to Abby, who cer-
emoniously carried them over to the corner of the
room where most of the boys sat. She proceeded to
tear each one in two. Then, as the form looked on,
she began to drop them, one broken heart at a
time, into the wastepaper bin.

Chapter 2

"So who do you think it is?"

Sulvinder and Lorna were in English, one of the classes that they didn't share with Abby. Miss Tate was explaining the structure of the Shakespearian sonnet for the umpteenth time. Lorna thought that she was wasting her time. Most of the boys in this class would find it hard to remember the structure of a limerick.

"How should I know?" Lorna replied. "I can't read minds."

"Do you think it might be Colin?"

The girls looked over at the shy, freckled boy who was answering Miss Tate's question about rhyming couplets. Lorna shrugged.

"I doubt it."

"How about Joe?"

Joe Green was a slim, good-looking boy who was always making "clever" quips during lessons.

"I hope not," said Lorna. "He's such a jerk."

Though she had to admit to herself that, if the

card was from Joe, she would feel flattered. She could fancy him, if he wasn't so irritating . . .

"How about Andy," Sulvinder went on. "Or Martin. . . ?"

"Puh-lease!"

The thing was, Lorna decided, while she liked being sent a romantic card, she hated the idea of it being from any of the boys she actually knew.

"Lorna, perhaps you can explain."

Lorna took a deep breath. She hated it when teachers asked her questions last of all, knowing that she'd get it right. It made her look like such a goody-goody. She couldn't help the fact that she was good at school.

"I'm sorry, Miss, I wasn't listening."

"The structural differences between a Petrarchan sonnet and a Shakespearian sonnet."

"The Petrarchan sonnet is the same as the Miltonic sonnet, except that you don't get a break between the octave and the sestet. There are only two rhymes in the octave and two or three in the sestet. The Shakespearian sonnet is much less strict. It's really three quatrains followed by a rhyming couplet."

"Very good."

As Lorna finished speaking, she heard a loud groan coming from the direction of Joe Green. Despite herself, she blushed.

"Stop that, Joe," Miss Tate ordered.

Joe grinned.

"Shall I compare thee to a micro-computer?" He asked, looking in Lorna's direction. "Thou hast more memory and efficiency."

"Get lost!" Lorna told him.

The lesson ended.

"I don't care who the card's from," Lorna told Sulvinder on the way to Chemistry. "They're all cretins. We're better off without them."

Lorna managed to put the card to the back of her mind during the rest of the day, concentrating on her classes. She managed to fit in ten pages of *The Tenant of Wildfell Hall* before the end of Maths. But the last lesson of the day was Media Studies, where everyone was trying to complete their Practical Project. Everyone, that is, except for Lorna, Abby and Sulvinder, who had all nearly finished, with a fortnight left before the deadline.

Abby was working on her own. She had made a video criticizing Westtown's lack of facilities for young people. She was now busy designing the cover for it. Lorna and Sulvinder were working together. They'd produced a radio magazine programme aimed at people of their age. They had finished all the taping, sound dubbing and mixing. All they had to do was finish writing the log which explained how they'd done it.

Across the room, Brian Kane had persuaded the teacher, Mrs Wright, to let him show a video he'd shot over the weekend. It was a film of a band led by one of his friends. The rest of the class, apart from the three girls, crowded round to watch it. Lorna glanced across the room now and then, when the others weren't looking, just to check it out. She could see that the camerawork was good, even if the music wasn't.

This irritated Lorna a little. Lorna didn't like to think that one of the boys might get as good a mark as her and Sulvinder. They had spent countless weekends researching the items on their show, followed by numerous lessons and lunchtimes recording and rerecording until they'd got it right.

When he'd finished showing the film, Brian took the tape over to the editing machine and began to work on the title for it. Lorna wandered over, pretending to be getting more paper for her log. Really, she was fascinated by the process of editing. Recently, she'd decided that her ambition was to be a TV journalist when she left university, and eventually, maybe, a documentary maker, responsible for writing her own scripts and editing the film, too.

"Do you want a go?" Brian asked, as Lorna looked over his shoulder. Embarrassed, she shook her head.

"I was just curious about why you're making this film," she told the long-haired boy. "I mean, I thought you'd already done a magazine about the . . . whatever you call it."

"The Indie scene," Brian said. "That's right. But this video is a free gift, to go with the first issue."

"Seems a bit extravagant to me," Lorna told him.

"Maybe. But it's my mate's band and I'm doing him a favour. All this gear will make them a fairly professional-looking video." He lowered his voice. "I'm going to run them off a load of copies to send to record companies. But don't tell Mrs Wright that."

Lorna found it hard to concentrate on writing up her log – that was the boring part. Instead, she got out her book and read it under the table, confident that Mrs Wright wouldn't notice and, even if she did, wouldn't do anything about it.

"Have you finished everything, Lorna?"

Lorna winced, embarrassed.

"Nearly. I was just taking a break."

Mrs Wright reached beneath the table and pulled out Lorna's book.

"Ah, *The Tenant of Wildfell Hall*. That used to be one of my favourites. Are you enjoying it?"

"It's OK," Lorna told the teacher. "Not as good as *Agnes Grey*."

"Where are you up to?"

"Helen's realizing what she's let herself in for by marrying Arthur, but she still loves him even though they're not that compatible. Mr Hargrave keeps chasing her, but she's not at all interested. She thinks that if she loves Arthur, everything will be all right."

"And what do you think?"

"Oh, they're bound to split up," Lorna said, "otherwise there wouldn't be a story. Only I wish that Anne Brontë would get on with it."

"Good stories can take time."

"I know," Lorna said. "But she should never have married him in the first place. It's obviously just an infatuation – she's so prim and proper, while he's so smug and sexy."

"But she was in love."

"Yes, but it can't have been true love, or. . . ."

The teacher smiled condescendingly.

"I think that 'true love' is over-rated. If I'd spent my whole life waiting for it, I'd be an old maid by now."

Mrs Wright smiled, and moved on to the group of giggly girls who were way behind with their work. Lorna discussed what she'd said with Sulvinder.

"Do you believe in true love?" she asked her friend.

"Sure. But it takes time to grow, after you're married. That's what my mum says, anyway."

"I can't accept that," Lorna told her. "Like, what Mrs Wright just said – she was almost admitting that she wasn't in love with her husband when she married him."

"Nonsense," Sulvinder told her. "I didn't hear what she said, but I'll bet that wasn't it."

"Not exactly," Lorna admitted. "But she did say that true love doesn't exist. I think she's wrong. Don't you?"

"You're a perfectionist," Sulvinder told her. "You want everything to be just right, or not at all. Love isn't the most important thing in the world. Not romantic love, anyway."

"Isn't it?" Lorna asked, more to herself than to her friend. But Sulvinder didn't reply, and both of them got out some notes to revise for the following week's mock exams.

"Let's see your card then."

Mum was late back from work. Lorna had

already made tea for herself and Ben, as Ric was taking Mum out to dinner.

"Here."

Unlike most of her friends, Lorna kept no secrets from her mum, but revealing the card embarrassed her.

"Very nice. Very romantic. So who's the boy with the good taste, then?"

"I've no idea."

"None at all?"

Lorna shook her head.

"You'd tell me if there was someone, wouldn't you?"

"Course I would."

Mum smiled reassuringly.

"Only, sometimes it seems like you take your schoolwork so seriously that you're missing out on the real world. It's easy to do, I know. I was the same when I was your age."

Lorna groaned to herself. First Mrs Wright, now Mum. She hated it when adults pulled that "When I was your age" stuff. As though things were the same then as they are now! At university, Mum met Dad, fell in love and, almost before she knew it, was pregnant with Lorna, living in a tiny flat with no money and a husband who resented being tied down even more than she did.

It took Mum an extra year to finish her degree and then, just as she was starting her PhD, Ben came along. To make matters worse, Dad walked out on her six months after Ben was born. Somehow, Mum coped. Now she worked part time at Westtown University (though she still called it "the poly"). She was fond of saying that, if she hadn't met Gary Haines, she might be a Cambridge Professor by now.

The doorbell rang, saving Lorna from more teenage reminiscences. Mum cursed.

"Why is he always early? Get that, would you, Lorna? I need to fix my face."

Lorna let Ric in. He was wearing a brown leather jacket which matched his hair, and Levi 501s.

"Lorna! How's my favourite teenager?"

Lorna smiled shyly. Ric always flirted with her in a way that she would never let boys at school get away with.

Ric followed her into the kitchen. Immediately, he picked up the Matisse card, which Mum, embarrassingly, had put next to hers.

"What's this?" Ric said, picking it up. "Have I got a rival for Kathy's affections?"

Lorna tried to grab it from him, but Ric, grinning, held it out of her reach.

"So I'm safe, am I? It's not your mother's. Go on, let me look."

Lorna said nothing, feeling like a little kid. Ric opened the card, read it, and raised his eyebrows.

"An anonymous admirer. Or do you. . . ?"

"No," said Lorna. "I don't."

She hoped that her face wasn't red. Somehow, it made her uncomfortable, Ric knowing about these first stirrings of romance in her life. It probably meant nothing, after all.

"Well," Ric said, "Whoever it's from, he's got

good taste. If I was nineteen, instead of twenty-nine, I reckon I'd have sent you one myself."

Lorna felt herself blushing, and had to go out of the room, leaving her card behind. It wasn't the first time that the thought had occurred to her. She and her friends had ruled out boyfriends for the time being, but that only applied to boys from Westtown Comp. If only Ric were nineteen, and did feel the way he said he felt, she would go out with him like a shot. But those were dangerous thoughts, so she got out her Chemistry textbook, and immersed herself in revision instead.

Chapter 3

Four months. That was all. Then Lorna would be rid of Westtown Comprehensive and everything that came with it. She could make a fresh start at the Sixth Form college. There was a small sixth form at the comp, but she had no intention of staying on there. Lorna couldn't stand the thought of another two years incarcerated with the people she'd spent the last five with. The next four months couldn't pass quickly enough, as far as she was concerned.

However, at the moment, time seemed to be slowing down. A week had gone by since Valentine's Day, and Lorna had given up trying to guess who her card was from. Most of the time she succeeded in forgetting about it. But not always. The main thing on her mind was the mocks. She had revised for them thoroughly, but, even so, she kept doing more. It was important to her that she did as well as everybody expected her to.

Lorna had nine days' worth of exams, covering

every subject except Media Studies, which was all coursework. The first five had gone well. Lorna never admitted it to anyone, but she quite enjoyed doing exams. Working under pressure suited her.

She and Sulvinder did all the same courses, so they spent evenings at each other's houses, revising together.

"I've been talking to Jazz in the sixth form," Sulvinder said, as they were taking a coffee break. "Do you know him?"

"I know who he is."

Jasvinder Jones had arrived at the school at the beginning of the academic year.

"He's having a party on Saturday, to celebrate his seventeenth birthday. He asked me if I'd go."

Lorna raised an eyebrow.

"And what did you say?"

"I said it depends."

"Depends on what?"

"He said to bring someone with me if I liked. I said whether I came would depend on if my friend would come too."

"I see."

Lorna thought for a moment. This was the first time she'd known Sulvinder show any interest in a boy, although plenty of them had tried to chat her up in the past. Usually, Sulvinder gave each boy such a polite brush-off that it was impossible for them to be offended.

"I'm not that good with parties," Lorna replied, eventually. "Why don't you take Abby? She likes dancing."

Sulvinder frowned.

"*You're* my best friend, not Abby. Anyway, I don't think Jazz likes her."

"How do you know that? Did he tell you?"

"No, but most of the older lads at school either fancy Abby like mad or can't stand her. They think she's really stuck up."

"They probably think the same about me."

Sulvinder was silent. It occurred to Lorna that she may have hit upon an uncomfortable truth.

"Please come," Sulvinder said.

Lorna hesitated. She felt uncomfortable at parties. There were only four things to do at them: talk, dance, drink or get off with somebody. She'd never been very good at small-talk. She felt self-conscious, dancing in public. As for alcohol, she only liked to drink in small quantities. She didn't want to risk being out of control. Anything could happen.

"We agreed," she said to Sulvinder. "No boyfriends until we're out of the Comp."

"Who said anything about boyfriends?" Sulvinder argued. "My parents would have a fit if I went out with anybody. I'm just talking about a party to celebrate the end of the mocks."

"I'll be bored," Lorna moaned, changing her tack, "and uncomfortable."

"In that case, we can leave early. But we deserve a night out after all these exams."

"I don't know."

"Maybe you'll discover who sent you that Valentine."

"If it's somebody from school who's going to be at Jazz's party, I'm not sure I want to know."

Sulvinder was silent. She knew how to get her way with Lorna — all she had to do was press her guilt buttons. If Lorna believed that she was responsible for making her friend unhappy, then she would cave in.

"Don't tell Abby," Lorna said, finally. "She'll think I've lost my mind."

"And what's wrong with losing your mind now and then?" Sulvinder asked. "You're only young once."

"Tell my mother that," Lorna suggested. "She acts more like a teenager than I do." She opened the Chemistry textbook and, before Sulvinder could reply, began to test her on chemical equations.

"A party?" Mum said. "Lucky you. Whose house is it at?"

"Just this lad at school. I don't really know him. He's Asian."

"Excellent," Mum said. "It'll do you good to widen your social circles."

Lorna was disappointed. Secretly, she'd been hoping that Mum would come on as the strict parent, refusing to let her go to the house of a boy she didn't know. But Mum was far too liberal for that.

"I think you could do with some new clothes," Mum told her. "Why don't I take you into town on Saturday?"

"You can't afford it."

"Don't tell me what I can or can't afford, young lady."

"But I've already had my clothing allowance."

"Yes. Your father pays that. But I like to treat you occasionally, too. I know what's really on your mind."

"What?"

"You don't want me choosing clothes with you. I can understand that. I'd feel the same."

Mum was right. It irritated Lorna when her mother was able to second-guess her.

"So I'll lend you my Oasis charge card. You can choose for yourself. All right?"

"All right. Thanks, Mum."

"You're welcome. And you're not the only one going to a party on Saturday night, so you won't be able to ring me up for a lift when you get tired of it. Make sure that you and Sulvinder have enough money to share a taxi. I don't want you bumming a ride off some drunken teenage boy with one thing on his mind."

"Ugh!" said Lorna. "Do you think I'm going to go crazy?"

"Not yet," Mum replied, "but there's always a first time."

Sulvinder and Lorna spent an hour in Oasis, trying on nearly everything in the shop, before Lorna settled on a long purple silk blouse, with swirly Indian-style embroidery around the bottom. It was expensive, but it would go with her black jeans and the boots her mother had bought her for Christmas, so she didn't need anything else.

"Look who it is!"

Abby was on the other side of the street, with

25

Melissa Harper. Both were carrying their badminton rackets. They must have just come from the sports centre.

"Got time for a coffee?"

Sulvinder and Lorna looked at each other. They could hardly refuse.

In the coffee bar, Lorna showed Abby her blouse.

"Let's have a look then — oh, that's gorgeous! It's so *you* ... I wish I could afford to shop there ..." Abby's voice trailed off. For a moment, she had let her guard slip. Abby didn't usually act sorry for herself. It was an unspoken thing she and Lorna had in common — there wasn't much spare money around at home.

"Heard from your dad recently?" Abby asked, changing the subject and probably guessing that the clothes money came from him.

Lorna didn't reply. Abby had never known her father. Lorna suspected that he had been married to someone else, but Abby avoided discussing the matter. However, she enjoyed getting Lorna to support her tirades against fathers, and men in general. Today, Lorna didn't feel like joining in, and there was an embarrassing silence.

"Lorna's mum's got a charge card at Oasis," Sulvinder revealed, smoothing things over the way she always did.

"What's the occasion?" Abby asked.

"Nothing in particular," Lorna replied, guardedly. But Abby wouldn't let the matter rest.

"Why's she lent you her card? Is she taking you out somewhere?"

Sulvinder answered.

"No. I am. I've been invited to a party by this boy I know."

Abby raised her eyebrows.

"What's his name?"

"Jazz."

"Do I know him?"

"He's in the sixth form. Half-Asian. Tall, quite light-skinned, with sideburns."

Abby shrugged and shook her head.

"So you and Lorna are going?" Melissa interrupted.

"Quite a few people in our year are going. I've heard people talking about it."

"I expect it would be all right if you two came," Sulvinder said. "He did say that I could bring a friend or two. I guess three would be all right."

Abby ummed and aahed, but Melissa, who didn't get invited to as many parties as she did, looked keen. Eventually Abby agreed to come, as though she were doing the rest of them a favour. Sulvinder told them the address and the two other girls went off, smiling.

"I'm surprised Abby wanted to come," Lorna said, when they'd gone.

Sulvinder seemed less surprised.

"A lot of people at school were angling for invitations to the party."

"Maybe. But Abby doesn't know who Jazz is."

"You can never tell with Abby," Sulvinder replied. "Sometimes she pretends not to know people because she thinks that she *shouldn't* know them. She might not know who Jazz is, but she probably knows his dad's name."

"Why?" Lorna asked, "Who exactly *is* Jazz's dad?"

"A bloke called Bill Jones. He directs programmes for Channel 4. He makes *The Company*, too."

The Company was a drama programme set in the business world, which got very high audience ratings. Lorna thought it was really just a glossy soap opera, but she found it compulsive viewing anyhow. She wondered if Sulvinder was right about Abby's reason for wangling the invitation. One thing was for sure, anything Abby did, she did for a reason.

Chapter 4

Lorna sat in her bedroom, feeling nervous. Who would be at the party tonight? She looked at herself in the mirror over the dressing table. Out of focus, she looked lovely — like one of those princesses in a children's picture book. But when she put her glasses on, it was a different story. Her round spectacles gave her a sterner, more mature appearance, but didn't disguise the fact that she looked young for her age. The other day, at school, a new teacher had confused her with someone in a class two years below her own.

Lorna had good skin, and well-kept blonde hair, but her figure had barely changed since primary school, and she had yet to reach five feet. At school, she could make up for her lack of physical maturity by outshining everyone in whatever subject she was studying. But at a party, where everyone usually managed to look older than they were, it might be another story. Still, she would have Sulvinder to protect her, not to mention Abby and Melissa. It might not be too bad.

To take her mind off it, Lorna got out some of her mother's old LP records. Lorna didn't have much time for music. Last year, however, Mum had bought a CD player and had given Lorna her record player and the pick of her old records before the rest went to the Oxfam shop. Lorna had chosen a bunch of classical LPs and some by singer/songwriters from the seventies. The latter were ones she remembered liking as a child. Mum used to play them when they were in the house on their own.

There was Laura Nyro, with her tortured, bluesy voice, and James Taylor, who sounded like warm, home-made honey. Now, though, Lorna chose a song by Janis Ian, *At Seventeen*, which suited her mood. It was all about girls who didn't get invited to parties and didn't get sent Valentines. Lorna identified with these girls, who spent their nights inventing lovers on the telephone to make themselves feel better.

Tonight, though, it didn't quite ring true. After all, someone *had* sent Lorna a Valentine card, and she *had* been invited to a party tonight, albeit at secondhand. And she didn't even have spots, like the singer of the song. Lorna wasn't an "ugly duckling". But she wasn't a swan, either.

There was a knock on her door.

"What are you playing that for?" Mum asked. "I haven't heard this record in years. I used to play Janis Ian a lot after your father left. I don't suppose you remember. Is *Stars* on the album? I love that song."

Before Lorna could reply, Mum went on.

"Anyway, get your coat. If you want me to give you and Sulvinder a lift to this party we'd better get going. Ric's coming to pick me up at nine."

"OK."

In the hallway, Lorna heard Mum giving Ben a lecture on his behaviour while she was out. At thirteen, Mum considered him just old enough to be left alone without a babysitter. Lorna wasn't sure she agreed. When Mum had finished, Lorna added her threats about what would happen if he so much as thought about going into her room.

"You look really nice," Mum said, as they drove to Sulvinder's house.

"So do you," Lorna replied.

It was true. Sometimes Lorna found it disconcerting to have a mother who, on her good days, could be mistaken for her elder sister.

"Is anyone special going to be at this party tonight?" Mum asked.

Lorna shook her head without speaking.

"And if there was, you wouldn't tell me, right?"

"There isn't."

They pulled up outside Sulvinder's house and Mum sounded the horn. When her friend got into the car, Lorna saw that, beneath her coat, Sulvinder was wearing dark crushed velvet flared jeans and an orange "body". She looked about twenty. They complimented each other on their appearance.

"I remember going to parties when I was your age," Mum said, from the driver's seat. "My friends and I, we used to size up all the boys who were available, decided which ones we fancied most, then deliberately insult them; you know, 'Where did you get that shirt – a jumble sale?' that kind of thing. If they argued back we knew we'd picked a winner. If they wimped out, we let them go. It's a good technique – you should try it."

"Mum, you're embarrassing me!" Lorna moaned.

Happily, at that point, they arrived at the house. It was a big one – almost a mansion as far as Lorna was concerned – on the edge of Coddington.

"Who lives here?" Mum asked. "A millionaire?"

"Jazz's father's name is Bill Jones," Sulvinder said.

"Oh, I've heard of him," Mum responded. "He used to direct a lot of plays for BBC2 – Ken Loach, Trevor Griffiths, people like that – very political. I didn't know he lived around here."

"Bill Jones produces *The Company*," Lorna said as she got out of the car, in a voice which implied that her mum was being impossibly ignorant.

"Never heard of it," Mum said. "But anyway, have a good time." She drove off as the front door opened, and the girls went inside.

Music thudded through the spacious house. There were people everywhere: some of them, Lorna was glad to see, quite a lot older than her. Jazz, a tall, handsome boy with thick sideburns, welcomed the girls in and contrived to give Sulvinder a small hug. He smiled at Lorna.

"Glad you could make it. I'm sure you'll know lots of people here."

"I'm sure."

Lorna took in her surroundings as Jazz went off with her coat. The walls were covered in pictures. Some of them were original paintings and there were a few framed film posters, but most of the pictures were photographs, which ranged from New York street scenes to nature studies.

"That's an original Ansel Adams," a slim Asian girl told Lorna. "My father's a big fan of his."

"Really?" Lorna asked, ashamed that she knew practically nothing about photography. She changed the subject.

"You don't go to Westtown Comp, do you?"

"No. I go to a private school. I'm Pamelajit, Jazz's sister."

"Lorna."

They talked for a while. Pamelajit was a bit younger than Lorna, but the two girls got on well. It was only after they'd been talking for fifteen minutes that Lorna realized Sulvinder hadn't returned from hanging up their coats with Jazz. She must still be with him. Lorna guessed that Jazz had shrewdly persuaded his younger sister to keep Lorna occupied. He must be keen on Sulvinder.

In the hall, Lorna joined Abby, who was talking to Amelia Gorman, a glamorous girl who used to go to Westtown Comp. Amelia was there with her boyfriend, Kevin, who was in Lorna's year.

"What are you doing here?" Lorna asked.

Amelia smiled her usual dazzling smile.

"I work as a PA for Jazz's dad," she said. "He's a friend of my father's."

That was Amelia for you, Lorna thought – only a string of mediocre GCSEs to her name but she'd managed to land a flash job in the media.

"Who *is* Jazz's dad?" Abby was curious.

"Didn't you know?" Lorna asked, surprised.

Before Abby could reply, Amelia gave the answer.

"He's a TV director. He makes *The Company* and various films for Channel 4. His name's Bill Jones."

"Bill Jones," Abby repeated.

"You must have heard of him."

Abby clearly had heard of him, but hadn't realized his connection with Jazz. She nodded, slowly.

"Yes," she said. "I certainly have."

Then, before Amelia could try to impress her further, Abby excused herself and wandered off. Lorna guessed that it was because she hated being upstaged, especially by someone as attractive as Amelia. Lorna had mixed feelings about Abby, but she always stuck by her friend. True, she could be snooty at times, and a bit overbearing, but she was smart, and interesting company. She could be very kind too, often when you least expected it.

For as long as Lorna could remember, Abby had kept a very tight circle of friends, which it was hard to gain admittance to. Melissa was the newest. Lorna had been her friend the longest, since the second year of primary school. They had never been quite "best" friends, but maybe that was why their friendship had survived for so long.

Abby could turn prickly like a hedgehog. She often fell out with people, but Lorna had become adept at smoothing things over with her.

Sulvinder was friendly with Abby too, but kept herself more at arm's length. Sulvinder's family had only moved to the area four years before, and this had made Abby wary of her at first. Abby didn't like anyone whose past she couldn't thoroughly dissect.

Now Abby returned to the hall and suggested to Lorna that they get a drink from the kitchen. She was wearing a lambswool black polo-neck with black leggings covered in pink spots. There was a single silver chain around her neck. Abby's mum wasn't well off, and Abby usually dressed simply, but this made her look more elegant, as far as Lorna was concerned. Admiring glances from boys at the party showed that they felt the same way. Abby was always making it clear that she wasn't interested in having a boyfriend, but that didn't stop boys from looking.

Ignoring the bottles spread out on the kitchen work surface, Abby opened the fridge door and pulled out a bottle of Chardonnay. Then she found a white wine glass and poured until it was half full. Replacing the wine in the fridge, she asked,

"Where's Sulvinder?"

"Good question," Lorna replied.

The two girls set off to explore the party. Sulvinder wasn't in the long living room, where Lorna had investigated the photographs. Nor was she in the hall. The next best bet was the basement, where the music was coming from.

They walked down the stairs cautiously. The space at the bottom of the house was a revelation. It wasn't a cellar. It was more like a purpose-designed party area. There was a CD jukebox in one corner, and a pinball machine in another. A barrel of beer stood at the bottom of the stairs and at the far end of the room was a sound system, with a DJ. In the middle of the room there were already quite a lot of people dancing. Sulvinder wasn't one of them.

"Hey, look who it is!"

Lorna turned round and groaned. There were three white boys from her year at school. She'd hoped that none of this group would be at the party. The speaker was Joe Green, the loud-mouth from her English group. At least Lorna was with Abby. She would take some of the heat off Lorna.

"You dancing, then?" Joe asked the girls. "Or are all the rumours about you lot true?"

"Of course we're dancing," Abby snapped back. "Why else would we be down here – to talk to you three?"

Now they were committed to having at least one dance, though Lorna would have preferred to find Sulvinder. They moved to the middle of the dance floor, followed by Joe Green and Mark Grey. Lorna felt uncomfortable dancing, especially to music she didn't know. To make matters worse, Joe began to dance opposite her.

"Who invited you here?" she asked him.

"Mark's sister, Jane, goes to the same school as Jazz's sister, Pamelajit. Pam asked Jane to bring a few younger lads. Who asked you?"

Lorna blushed, realizing that the connection which had got her invited to the party was just as tenuous as his, but before she could come up with an answer, Joe spoke again.

"I didn't think you came out at night. I thought you spent all your time studying."

"Ha, ha!" Lorna replied, sarcastically.

"No, seriously," Joe said. "You look nice. Seeing you like this tonight has made me see you in a new light."

Lorna couldn't tell if he was being entirely sarcastic or not. She would have liked to walk away, but she knew something about the etiquette of dancing. Leaving mid-song – even if you didn't like your partner – just wasn't on.

"What I can't understand," Joe said, still sounding serious, though it was hard to be sure, because he was having to raise his voice to be heard above the music, "is why you hang around with Abigail Thomas. I mean, you're not really like her, are you?"

Lorna stopped dancing.

"Look," she said, shouting in Joe's ear. "I don't like you and I know you don't like me. So why don't you try and find a girl who'll be impressed by your adolescent sneering and leave me to have a good time."

Joe appeared hurt. He was rather good looking, Lorna had to admit to herself, and it was just possible that he hadn't meant to offend her. But the fact that she might fancy him made the whole scenario worse. So, without saying anything to Abby, she walked off the dance floor and back up the stairs to the rest of the party.

Chapter 5

Sulvinder was still nowhere to be seen, so Lorna went to the first floor. There were more photographs on the wall, and a big landing. But she couldn't see anybody. This was an area not being used for the party. She was about to go back downstairs when she noticed a door, slightly ajar. She walked over to it quietly. Coats were strewn over the bed. That was all it was: an overflow cloakroom.

As she was turning away, Lorna heard voices. She couldn't be sure about the male one, but the female one was her friend's. Sulvinder was saying "Yes. Maybe. I'd have to ask. Really?"

Then she laughed and used Jazz's name. Lorna felt a buzz of jealousy. It wasn't right. Asian girls were meant to avoid romance. They had all those family taboos. But here was her best friend, being courted intently by a good-looking, rich boy, leaving Lorna to fend for herself. Not wanting to be a voyeur, Lorna went quickly downstairs.

She wandered into the living room and began to look at the pictures again, hoping someone would come up to her and talk. But no one did. They all had a more interesting person to talk to. Maybe Mel or Abby would surface shortly. They could have a good gossip about who was at the party, and who they were with. That sort of thing didn't interest Lorna all that much, really, but when Abby talked about it, it was fun, like a tacky soap opera.

But neither of them came. Maybe both girls were enjoying themselves dancing. Lorna stood on her own, finishing her drink. She stared long and hard at a photograph by somebody called Weegee, which showed what seemed like a million people, all crowded together on a beach, staring at the camera. I wish I were somewhere else, she thought. I wish I were anywhere else in the world but here.

"Penny for them."

Lorna looked round in irritation, recognizing the voice of Joe Green.

"What do you reckon to the party?" Joe asked, politely.

"It's OK."

"I didn't think it was your kind of thing."

"Why not?" Lorna snapped at him. "I suppose just because I'm good at school you think I don't know how to enjoy myself."

"I didn't mean that," Joe replied. "I'm sorry. I really am. I didn't mean to get at you. I shouldn't have slagged off your friend, either. I expect she's all right if you get to know her. Look, let me get you a drink, make amends. All right?"

"All right," said Lorna.

She stood beside the picture, waiting for him to come back. She didn't like Joe, but she liked being on her own at the party even less. It was comforting to have a good-looking boy paying attention to her, even if he was a jerk.

Joe returned with a beer in one hand and a wine glass in the other.

"I forgot to ask," he said, "so I tried to figure what you were most likely to drink. I got you white wine and soda. Is that OK?"

"Fine."

Lorna didn't like alcohol much, but this drink tasted more like fizzy pop. She enjoyed it.

"Where's Sulvinder?" Joe asked. "I thought you two were like siamese twins."

"Well, you were wrong," Lorna insisted, sullenly. "She's around."

Joe looked abashed.

"Why have you got it in for me?" he asked, in a hurt tone of voice. "I'm only trying to be friendly."

Lorna's eyes blazed.

"What do you mean, 'Why have I got it in for *you*'? You're the one who's always teasing me in class. What was it you said the other day? That I'd got a *brain like a pocket calculator*?"

"I didn't say that."

"Something like it, anyway."

Joe shrugged.

"If I did, I'm sorry. It's just that, well, you're always the one who has the correct answer to everything. Now me, I'm just Joe Average, but it gets to me now and then, being shown up all the time."

Lorna responded angrily.

"And how do you think it makes me feel, always being asked last because Miss thinks I'll have the right answer? Do you think I like looking like a creep? I can't help it, you know – being good at school. What do you think I should do – get the answers wrong on purpose?"

Joe laughed. His eyes twinkled.

"Yeah, maybe that would be a good idea, just now and then. It'd do wonders for your image."

Now Lorna laughed, too.

"Here, let me get you another drink."

Lorna followed him into the kitchen, surprised that she'd drunk the first one so quickly. As they crossed the hall, she bumped into Pamelajit.

"Have you seen Jazz?" the Asian girl asked.

"I think he's upstairs, talking to Sulvinder."

"Not much of a host, is he?" Jazz's sister quipped.

Then she called and began to ascend the stairs. Lorna hoped she hadn't been stupid in telling her where her brother was. Suppose she interrupted them doing something . . . But *Sulvinder* . . . No, it was unthinkable.

Joe handed Lorna another drink. It was a little stronger than the last one, but slipped down just as easily.

"Friends?"

Lorna hesitated. She still thought that Joe might be winding her up – being friendly in order to turn on her afterwards and make fun of her in front of his friends, and hers. She was wary of making an embarrassing mistake. Then she saw his smile and relaxed.

"Friends."

Joe began telling stories about some of the other people at the school, including the boys he'd come to the party with. Lorna found herself laughing a lot. She'd thought of those boys as immature, arrogant adolescents. But Joe made his friends sound like characters in a situation comedy. They were always trying to act like they were older than they really were. Instead of looking cool, they made fools of themselves. Lorna ought to be sorry for them really. Joe raised his glass.

"Jazz! Great party!"

"Glad you could make it."

So Pamelajit had brought Jazz out of hiding. But where was Sulvinder? As Lorna glanced around, Abby came out of the basement. Lorna felt a twinge of embarrassment. What would Abby say if she saw her talking to Joe? But, as it happened, Abby seemed more intent on straightening up her appearance, and headed straight for the bathroom.

Lorna tried to think of something to say to Joe, before he realized how boring she was and walked away. But nothing came to mind. Instead, she found herself asking, "If I promise not to desert you this time, do you want to dance again?"

Joe smiled, with a twinkle in his eye.

"Go on then."

He refilled their drinks before they went down.

The dance floor was crowded and the music was louder than before. At the far end of the room, couples were kissing and canoodling. Lorna's glasses steamed up and she put them into the pocket of her blouse. Joe seemed to be staring at her. Lorna blinked at him. She was quite short sighted and his face had became a little fuzzy, which made it all the more endearing. They began to dance.

"Hey," he shouted, above the throbbing music, "I've never seen you without your specs on before. You're really beautiful, did anyone ever tell you that?"

Lorna blushed. It wasn't true, she knew. It was the low light and the drink and the music. Still, this was the first time that she'd been called beautiful by someone she wasn't related to. Eventually she replied, not shouting, but calling into his ear.

"Thanks," she said. "You're not so bad yourself." They continued dancing.

Without her glasses on, Lorna felt a kind of freedom. She could no longer see who was in the room, so she couldn't worry about what they thought of her. If some people were giggling at the sight of such a mis-matched couple, she couldn't tell. And she felt attractive tonight.

As the evening wore on, more people arrived. Jazz seemed to have invited the entire sixth form, and there were quite a few people from Lorna's year. A few of them got close enough for her to recognize them. One was Brian Kane, the long-haired boy from her tutor group.

"Lorna!" he said. "You look terrific. I didn't recognize you at first. Do you want to dance?"

Just as he finished speaking, Joe returned with fresh drinks.

"Sorry," she told Brian. "I'm with Joe."

Brian looked at her, then at Joe, as if he thought she was joking. Then he walked away, looking confused. Joe put the drinks down on a table near the corner. Pressure of numbers was forcing them to the far end of the room, where couples were canoodling.

Lorna didn't want Joe to get the wrong idea. He was being nice tonight, but that didn't mean she'd stop finding him irritating at school. She certainly wasn't going to ... but now the music seemed to be slowing down. As a ballad came on, Joe awkwardly put his arms around her waist. Lorna did the same, pressing her body lightly against his. Her skin began to tingle with pleasure. She couldn't remember when she had last felt this relaxed. She had certainly never felt so aroused before. It was a wonderful sensation.

I must have been mad, she told herself, wanting to keep away from boys, if it can make you feel like this. But maybe it wasn't just boys, she realized. Maybe it was this one particular boy. She wondered if he really liked her, or if he was with her out of kindness, because he'd seen her on her own.

Lorna's head was on a level with the top of Joe's neck. It was easy for him to lean down and whisper into her ear. As he did, their bodies pressed closer together. His hands moved a little lower, sending sexy shivers down her spine.

"Did you mean it," he asked, "when you told Brian you were with me?"

"What else could I have meant?"

Joe didn't reply. The song ended, but neither of them moved. They were alone, in the darkest corner of the room, but it seemed like there was a glow around them. Lorna didn't want to move away from him, didn't want to lose the feeling of his warm body pressing against hers. Because, if he did move away, the spell might be broken. Both of them might remember that, an hour ago, they couldn't stand each other.

"You know . . ." Joe whispered, his breath hot on her ears, "I'm still a bit frightened of you."

Lorna was moved. It hadn't occurred to her that he might be feeling as vulnerable as she was. She stood on tiptoe and whispered into his ear.

"You shouldn't be. Really. I don't bite."

"Honest? Do you promise not to set me an examination on how to be an ideal boyfriend?"

Lorna smiled confidently, but her heart was trembling. She couldn't believe that he was asking her to go out with him. She almost felt like crying.

"I promise."

Joe gazed into her eyes and smiled.

"So what do I do now?"

Lorna smiled back. There was only one thing they could do. She opened her mouth, and, as she began to speak, wondered how far she was going to fall — knowing that, once their lips met, nothing would ever be the same again. She answered his question.

"Kiss me, stupid."

And he did.

Chapter 6

The party was breaking up and Lorna was still in Joe's arms. They hadn't had a drink for hours, yet still she felt intoxicated. It was the effect of the kisses and caresses and the soft words he whispered in her ear. Lorna's head was spinning and she didn't want it to stop.

They hadn't talked very much. Mainly, it seemed, they talked about how much they'd disliked each other until this evening. Vaguely, Lorna remembered what Mum had been saying to her in the car on the way to the party – something about the best way to choose a man was to find one you could have a good argument with. Now and then, it seemed, her mother got it right.

Someone tapped her shoulder. Lorna turned round. Sulvinder.

"So this is where you disappeared to. I thought you'd gone home."

Lorna laughed as Sulvinder said hello to Joe.

"What do you mean – 'disappeared'? You're the

one who vanished within seconds of us arriving."

Now it was Sulvinder's turn to look embarrassed.

"I'm sorry. I'll tell you all about it in the taxi."

"Taxi?"

"Yes, I've just ordered one. Have you seen the time? My dad's going to murder me!"

Lorna put on her glasses and looked at her watch. It was nearly one.

"We'd better find our coats," she said to Sulvinder. Then, to Joe, "Can we give you a lift home?"

"It's OK. I'll walk. It's not far."

Joe came upstairs with them. As they got to the top of the basement steps, Lorna asked, "Are Mel and Abby still here?"

"You're kidding! They left over an hour ago."

"Did they. . . ?"

"See you and lover-boy? I don't think so. But they were curious about where you'd disappeared to. Come to think of it, they were curious about where I'd disappeared to, too."

At the door, Joe and Lorna kissed until the taxi arrived. He looked even more handsome in the moonlight. Lorna felt like the luckiest girl in the world.

"I'll call you tomorrow," he said, as the taxi pulled up. "What's your number?"

It was in the book, but Lorna told him anyhow.

"555 0945," she said. "Don't forget."

"I won't," he promised. "I'll memorize it as I walk home."

As they got into the car they heard him repeating "555 0945", "555 0945", "555 . . ."

* * *

49

As soon as they had put their seat belts on and told the driver where they were going the two girls looked at each other and giggled.

"I thought you couldn't stand him!" Sulvinder said.

"So did I."

"You know that rule we made – the one about no boys until after the GCSEs? What are we going to do about it?"

"I don't know," Lorna replied. "Everything's different now, for me, anyway. But what about you? What happened with Jazz?"

Sulvinder looked embarrassed.

"How do you mean, *what happened*? Nothing happened. We just talked – that's all. I'm not like you, saying boys disgust me one minute, then falling over the first good-looking one who gets you drunk."

"I was *not* drunk!"

Sulvinder laughed.

"You might not be drunk, but you look like you're on something."

"Come on," Lorna pleaded. "Tell me about you and Jazz."

"There's not a lot *to* tell," Sulvinder replied. "We sat upstairs and talked – you know, about this and that, things we liked – trying to find out if we liked each other."

"He didn't do anything?"

Sulvinder shook her head.

"It's not as easy as that, not if we're serious. I wouldn't respect him if he tried to . . . you know . . . and he wouldn't respect me if I let him. We have to go very slowly, not like you and Joe. You seemed to be in the fast lane."

"He is nice, isn't he?" Lorna asked.

"I don't have an opinion one way or the other," Sulvinder replied, diplomatically. "If you like him, I like him."

The taxi dropped Sulvinder off first. The house lights were still on. Lorna knew that her friend was going to be in big, big trouble.

"Tell them it was all my fault," she said, as Sulvinder got out. "Use whatever story you like. I'm sorry."

"No, you're not," Sulvinder said. "And neither am I."

In her room, Lorna spent half an hour writing her diary. But she couldn't sleep for ages, thinking about Joe. When would he call? Would he still be as keen on her tomorrow? How did she really feel about him? There were no answers to these questions, but they kept her awake nonetheless. Her mind was flooded with new thoughts and sensations. As she drifted off to sleep, it seemed that she was on the threshold of a great happiness, but there was a chasm of uncertainty beneath her. On the other side of it stood Joe, smiling.

Chapter 7

It was after ten when Lorna woke. The house was quiet. She put on her dressing gown, then went to the bathroom for a shower. The events of the previous night seemed like a dream. She was in a kind of daze, but, in one corner of her brain, a red light was flashing on and off. All of Lorna's cynical, self-critical side seemed to be warning her: *he didn't mean anything he said. Just watch. He'll back away.*

But she wouldn't let self-doubt win this morning. As the steaming hot water poured down her back, she felt renewed, alive in a way she'd never been before. She began singing an Indigo Girls song to herself — *Love will come to you.* When she'd first heard the song, it had sounded like a distant promise, farther away than America, more distant in time than university. But now it was beginning.

Lorna tried to exercise caution. Don't let yourself fall so far, so fast, she insisted to herself. But it didn't work. She dried off slowly, peering shortsightedly at her face in the steamed-up mirror, wondering whether Joe would think as much of it in the clear light of day.

The bathroom door opened to reveal Ric's face.

"Oh, sorry," he said. "I thought you were out of here."

"My fault. I forgot to bolt the door. I'll only be a minute."

Ric smiled apologetically. At least, Lorna thought that the smile was apologetic – without her glasses on, she couldn't really make out his expression. After giving him a few seconds to get out of her way, she went back to her bedroom and got dressed. Then she spent ten minutes brushing her hair. It was silly, but now she could admit it to herself. For the last six months, since he started getting serious with Mum, Lorna had had a bit of a crush on Ric. He was everything that the boys at school weren't: mature, handsome, intelligent. He talked to her about books and films as though she were an equal.

Lorna had behaved a little like one of the characters in the Victorian melodramas she was so fond of. She had been jealous of her own mother – a ridiculous, silly feeling, but she couldn't help it at the time. Now it was over. If Ric had walked in on Lorna like that a week ago, she would have spent hours brooding about it. This morning, the only person who kept returning to her mind was Joe.

When would he ring? It was too early yet, barely eleven. But maybe by twelve, or one? And why had she let him say that *he* would ring *her*?

Lorna, after all, was a feminist. She had as much right to ring the boy first, if she wanted. Nevertheless, she did want Joe to ring her first. But she wouldn't be able to relax properly until he had done.

"Good party?" Mum asked. She was drinking black coffee, a sure sign that she had a hangover.

"It was, actually," Lorna replied. "How about yours?"

"Passable. I'm getting a bit old for staying up till two. What time did you get in?"

Lorna shrugged.

"After midnight."

Mum didn't have a chance to question her further as, at that moment, Ric came in, smiling broadly.

"So how are my two favourite ladies this beautiful morning?"

Mum glanced out of the window.

"It looks rather overcast to me. Help yourself to breakfast."

The phone rang. Leaving her muesli, Lorna charged into the hall to answer it.

"Hello?"

"Hi, Lorna. It's me."

Abby.

"Hi."

"What happened to you last night? One minute you were on the dance floor, the next you were gone. We never saw you again."

Lorna avoided the question.

"Sulvinder said you left early," she said to Abby.

"Not that early. Anyway, I want to get out of the house this morning. My mother's got the entire

church social committee coming over afte
service. All right if I come over?"

"I guess . . ." Lorna was reluctant. "I'm j
finishing breakfast."

"My, you must have got to bed late!" Abby
teased. "You're usually halfway through your
homework by now. I'll see you in twenty minutes."

Before Lorna could think of an excuse, Abby had
hung up. Lorna returned to the kitchen.

"A boy?" Ric asked, with a grin.

"Why should it be?" Lorna retorted.

"You ran to that phone quick enough."

"Who was it?" Mum asked, in a low-key voice.

"Abby. She's coming round in a bit."

Mum groaned.

"On Sunday morning? Can't we ever have this
house to ourselves?"

"I'll take her up to my room. She has to get out
of the house. Her mum's got some church committee coming round."

Mum seemed more sympathetic.

"I suppose you two want to go over all the events
at that party you went to last night. There *were*
events, I take it?"

"There are always events," Lorna replied,
mysteriously. Before Mum could ask her any more
questions, she washed up her cereal bowl and
went upstairs.

Which would happen first — Abby arriving or Joe
ringing? Suppose Abby arrived while Joe was on
the phone? What would Lorna tell her? Maybe
Abby already knew about her and Joe. After all,

they had been at the same party. But Lorna had been in a dark corner of a large room. Abby would only know about Joe if someone had told her. And Abby was very choosy about who she did and didn't talk to.

"So your mum's still going out with *him*?" Abby asked, as she curled up on a cushion in the corner of Lorna's room. "How long is it now?"

"Six, seven months."

"You think they'll . . . you know?"

"My mum always says that she'll never get married again. She doesn't believe in it."

"Or she doesn't believe that anyone'll ever ask her," Abby said.

Lorna didn't reply. Abby always outdid her in the cynicism stakes. At least her friend hadn't gone on and on about the party yet.

"What about *your* mum?" Lorna asked. "Do you think she'd. . . ?" It wasn't the sort of question Lorna usually asked Abby, but she'd started this line of conversation.

"The way my father treated Mum put her off men for life," Abby muttered. Then she put on her usual, more casual tone.

"Occasionally some grotesque old widower she's met at church starts to come round, but she soon bores him to death by going on and on about the moral degeneration of society."

Lorna laughed. Abby, however, obviously didn't think that what she'd said was very funny.

"I think Sulvinder's lot have got it right. You know – arranged marriages. No looking around for the perfect person. You're not expected to fall in love with them until after you've been married. And no divorce either." Abby looked pensive.

"I'm not sure it always works out as simply as that," Lorna replied.

"What happened with Sulvinder last night?" Abby asked, perking up. "You two weren't hanging out together, were you?"

"We're not joined at the hip, you know," Lorna retorted.

"Oh, you mean like Mel and I are?"

"I didn't . . ."

"OK, OK . . . but I hardly saw you, and Sulvinder had a strange look about her – like there was something going on."

"You'd better ask her then."

Abby played with her rich, flowing hair.

"You're holding out on me, aren't you, Lorna? I think there's something you're not telling."

"Well, if you *will* leave early . . ." Lorna teased.

"Come on," said Abby. "What else happened?"

Before Lorna could reply, the telephone rang.

"Excuse me."

She hurried out of the room, but Mum had beaten her to it.

"Yes, I'll get her."

Mum looked up the stair well.

"For you. Sulvinder."

Lorna sighed.

"Has he called you yet?" Sulvinder asked.

"No. I thought you might be him. Has *he* called you?"

"You must be kidding! He'd never call me at home. Especially not today. I'm in all kinds of trouble for coming in so late last night. I've been grounded for a week."

"Didn't you tell your mum and dad that it was my fault?"

"Lorna, no one would ever believe that anything was ever your fault. Anyway, I could hardly tell them about you and Joe. They might start thinking that you weren't such a suitable friend for . . ." Suddenly there was a voice in the background and Sulvinder changed the subject.

"So the homework's not due till Tuesday? Thanks."

The conversation ended abruptly. Back upstairs, Lorna told Abby,

"That was Sulvinder. She's been grounded."

"Do you think we should go round and see her?"

"Can't. She's only allowed one friend at a time."

Abby returned to the subject of the party.

"So why did you stay so late?" Abby asked. "You looked bored when I arrived."

"Did I? I wasn't really. I had a good time – I talked to lots of people, danced a little . . ."

"I saw you giving that creep Joe Green a mouthful," Abby said.

"Yes," said Lorna, trying not to show her amusement. "I did." But not in the way you mean, she thought.

"Who did you talk to?"

"Oh, some of the other people there. Jazz's sister, for instance."

"Pamelajit?"

"Yes. She's nice."

"She is," Abby agreed. Then she said, more tentatively, "You know, I got the impression that her brother's keen on Sulvinder."

"Did you?" Lorna asked. "I don't know. But I guess, even if he was, they wouldn't be allowed to do anything about it, what with their religion and all."

"Sulvinder may be very religious," Abby said, "but I don't think Jazz is. He doesn't wear a turban, after all."

"Not all Sikhs do. Anyway, his dad's white, so maybe he isn't expected to."

"Maybe," Abby replied, thoughtfully.

It was after one. Abby stood up to go. As she did, the phone rang again. Lorna felt the hairs on her neck begin to bristle.

"Lorna, for you *again*," Mum called up the stairs.

"I'd better be going," Abby said, picking up her bag. "I'll be late for lunch."

"OK," Lorna told her, seeing her friend to the door.

The phone sat up-ended on the table in the middle of the hall.

"Aren't you going to pick that up?" Mum called from the kitchen.

"See you tomorrow," Abby said, as Lorna opened the door.

"Yes," said Lorna, pushing the door closed immediately behind her. "Tomorrow."

As she turned round she saw that Mum was standing in the kitchen doorway.

"You don't want to keep your caller waiting," she said, with an amused smile on her face. "It's a boy."

Chapter 8

"I was wondering," Joe said, with a smile in his voice, "whether you wanted me to come round and help you with your homework."

Lorna giggled.

"You're too late. I finished it all yesterday," she lied.

"Can I come over anyway?"

"Well . . ."

Lorna knew what she was supposed to do. She'd read enough books on the subject. Play a little hard to get. Don't let him take your time for granted. He'll want you more if you make him wait. But she couldn't start scheming. She wanted to see him now, this minute. She needed to.

"It might be best if you left it a little while. My mum's boyfriend's still here. I think they're going out later."

Lorna hoped that Mum and Ric *were* going out later. They often had a pub lunch on Sundays, since Mum couldn't be bothered to cook the traditional meal. Lorna didn't want Joe to have to meet either of them, not yet. Not if they could avoid it.

"I'll tell you what," Joe said. "The weather looks like it's brightening up. Why don't we meet for a walk in the copse?"

The copse was a small wood in between West-town and Coddington, the village where Joe lived. Lorna could be there in twenty minutes.

"That's a nice idea," she told him. "When?"

"How about now? I mean . . . I could meet you in a quarter of an hour."

"Better make it half an hour," Lorna said.

She needed time to get ready and to have at least two panics about what to wear.

"I'm not sure if I can wait that long," Joe told her.

"Me neither," Lorna breathed.

"Shouldn't that be 'neither can I'?" Joe teased her.

"I don't know," Lorna said. "And I don't care either. See you in half an hour." She put the phone down.

What to wear? It was a blustery day. Clouds were moving quickly through the sky. Her old jeans and a heavy sweater would be sensible for walking in the woods in this weather, but Lorna didn't feel sensible. She got out a soft cotton T-shirt which made her feel attractive and changed into the tight jeans she'd worn the night before. Downstairs, she reluctantly put on her walking shoes and duffle coat, spoiling the effect some-what.

"Going somewhere?" Ric grinned at her over the *Observer*.

"Just for a walk."

"Your mum and I are going out to lunch in half an hour. To 'The Boar', I think. Want to come with us?"

Lorna shook her head.

"I'll fix myself something when I get back."

"OK. See you later."

"Yes. 'Bye!"

Lorna left the house, glad to have missed her mum, who would have questioned her more closely. She looked at her watch. There were twenty-two minutes before she was due to meet Joe. She wouldn't be late.

Nevertheless, she walked quickly. All sorts of things were going through her mind. The thoughts moved so quickly that it was hard to focus on a single one. Was Joe older than her or younger? Would he find her as attractive in the daylight? Had he had a girlfriend before? If he had, Lorna hadn't noticed. But, then, why should she have noticed? She hadn't been interested in him before last night.

What sorts of things would they do together? Would he get on with her friends? Abby – probably not. But what did Sulvinder really make of him? Come to think of it, what did Lorna really think of Joe? Until last night she'd thought of him as an irritant, though she couldn't put her finger on anything really bad that he'd done. He was just another boy who had drifted in and out of view during her four-and-a-half years at Westtown Comp.

Would he be waiting for her when she arrived? As Lorna got closer to the copse this became a crucial question. Joe lived slightly nearer to the wood than she did, therefore he should be the first to arrive. But Lorna had noticed that the people who lived nearest to the school were always the ones who were late. Maybe there was some kind of reverse equation at work which meant . . . but there she went again, getting all intellectual about things. She mustn't say that sort of thing in front of Joe. He'd think she was showing off.

The road twisted round and the copse came into view. Lorna saw a figure in navy jeans and a red blouson, standing by the stile which led into it. He looked nervous, as though he wasn't sure that she would come. But then he looked in Lorna's direction. Seeing her, he raised his hand and gave her half a wave. Lorna took her hand out of her pocket and gave him the same wave. As she did, a cloud blew away from the sun and bright sunshine filled the air, momentarily blinding her.

When Lorna could see again, Joe was walking towards her. She didn't have time to wonder about whether he liked the way she looked or not. Awkwardly, they smiled at each other. Then they were in each other's arms, embracing. They kissed for a long time, as though they had been reunited after a long separation. All of Lorna's doubts disappeared. She wanted the moment to last forever. For a while, it seemed as if it would.

Slowly, they pulled apart. Joe took her hand and squeezed it gently.

"Shall we walk?"

"Why not?"

Spring seemed to be beginning. There were bluebells in the woods and the trees were coming into leaf, but Lorna only had eyes for Joe. He, too, kept staring at her.

"I don't quite believe this," she said, as they took a small twisting path on which they were unlikely to run into anybody.

"Me neither," Joe replied. "If someone had told me before the party yesterday that by the end of the evening I'd be going out with Lorna Haines, I'd have thought someone had spiked their drink."

Lorna laughed.

"So you didn't. . . ?"

"I knew I fancied you. But I'd never have thought of asking you out. I didn't think you'd be interested."

That didn't stop you sending me a Valentine's card, Lorna thought. But she wasn't going to be foolish enough to mention the card, in case it embarrassed Joe. They kissed again. Lorna's glasses steamed up, so she took them off.

"I was blind but now I can see," Joe quipped.

"More the other way round in my case," Lorna replied. "Don't let me walk into anything."

"Why don't you wear contacts?" Joe asked. "It's a shame to hide your gorgeous eyes."

Lorna blushed.

"Only vain people wear contact lenses," she said. "Anyway, I don't like the idea of putting bits of plastic into my eyes."

"Fair enough," Joe replied. "Just a suggestion."

"What do your friends think," she asked him, "about you going out with me?"

"I got one or two strange looks last night," he admitted, "but who cares what they think? Other people's opinions aren't important. It's how *we* feel that matters."

"I couldn't have put it better myself," Lorna said.

They'd nearly reached the end of the copse. Joe found a small grassy patch between two trees and they sat down there. The ground was slightly damp, but neither of them cared. The stains on Lorna's new jeans would wash out. They kissed and cuddled without talking much. After a while Lorna's stomach gave a loud grumble.

"Was that me or you?" Joe asked.

"Me, I'm afraid," Lorna admitted. "I didn't have much breakfast. Would you like to come back to the house for some lunch?"

"Er . . ."

"It's OK. Mum and Ric'll be out."

"Fine."

They walked slowly out of the wood and back towards the house. It had to be slow because Joe had his arm round her waist and hers was round his. You couldn't, Lorna discovered, walk quickly that way, but it didn't matter. The hunger seemed to vanish. She felt as if she was in one of those slushy movies, where couples keep gazing into each other's eyes as the sun sets behind them.

Only this wasn't a movie. This was real, and every few yards, it seemed, they would stop and kiss again. Joe was so good looking, so gentle and warm, Lorna had to keep kissing him to remind herself that he was hers.

"You've got a funny taste in music," Joe said, sorting through Lorna's LPs.

"They used to be my mum's," she explained. "Most of them are really old. The stuff I bought myself is all on cassette."

"I like this one." He held up k d lang's *Ingénue* album, which was full of love songs.

"Me too," Lorna said, and put it on.

It was only when the first side of the LP ended that they noticed the phone ringing.

"I'd better get that," Lorna said, sitting up.

"Can't you leave it?" Joe complained.

"The one time I left it would be the time that someone died, or was in hospital. I'm superstitious about things like that."

"I can't see you being *superstitious*. Don't you mean chronically sensible?" Joe teased, as Lorna left the room.

The way the phone kept ringing made Lorna sure it must be something important. She was walking on air as she answered it. She hoped that whatever it was wouldn't bring her back to earth. A familiar mid-Atlantic accent reassured her.

"Hello, sweetheart! I was just about to hang up."

"Hi, Dad! Sorry. I had loud music on."

"You? Loud music? Whatever next? Boyfriends? Drugs? Violent crime?"

Lorna laughed.

"Certainly not. Well, maybe the first one."

"You *are* growing up. Listen, kid, I'm sorry I haven't been in touch for so long. I'm going to make it up to you."

Lorna's father was a freelance financial consultant. He was based in the United States, but worked all over the world. Lorna wouldn't see him from one year to the next, but every so often he would show up with expensive presents. Or he would whisk her and Ben off for a weekend somewhere. The last time she'd heard from Dad, he'd revealed that he was about to divorce for the third time. Lorna and Ben, however, were his only children.

"How's Benny Boy?"

"Ben's thirteen, Dad. He's hardly a boy. I've no idea where he is, but since he didn't answer the phone, I assume he's out."

"Pity. You see, I've got a proposition that I want to put to both of you."

"What kind of proposition?"

"The thing is, I've landed myself a nice cushy contract for the next six months, setting up an accounting system for a chain of computer stores across the States."

Dad had lived in the USA for the last five years. Occasionally, he talked about Lorna and Ben visiting him, but nothing ever came of it.

"I've fixed it so that I'm going to be spending most of July and August in California – not too busy – I've factored in plenty of free time. And I figured that I owe you two a holiday. You're gonna need one, after all those exams you'll have done. What do you say, Lorna? San Francisco? The Pacific Coast highway in an open-top car? A chance to get to know your old man before he goes completely senile."

Lorna paused for thought.

"Are you still there?"

"I don't know," Lorna said. "I might have other plans."

"Other plans . . . how can you . . ." Dad sounded irritated for a moment, then his voice changed. "Hold on, I get it. Don't tell me. You're in love."

"Maybe," Lorna said. "What makes you say that?"

"You've been after me to bring you over in the summer for five years. So either you've finally worked out what a horrible person I am — which wouldn't surprise me — or there's somebody you'd rather be with. I'm hoping it's the latter. Am I right?"

"You're right," Lorna said. "But please don't tell Mum or Ben. They don't know anything about it yet."

"How long ago did all of this happen?"

"Last night."

"I see. What's the lucky boy's name?"

"Joe. He's in some of my classes at school."

"OK, Lorna. Don't worry about Joe. Just make sure he treats you right. If you're still seeing him in the summer, maybe you can bring him over for a while too. We don't need to make any arrangements just yet."

"If you say so."

Dad never needed to make any arrangements

yet. By the time he got round to thinking about arrangements, it was always too late.

"How's your mother? Still dating that lecturer guy?"

"They're out together now."

"Good for her. Give her my best, will you? And Ben too. Tell him to write me a letter, giving end-of-term dates and all that stuff. This time I'm serious; you tell him that."

"I'll tell him."

"This Joe guy — he's there at the moment, right?"

"How can you tell?"

"I can hear it in your voice. I'll let you get back to him. *Ciao*, baby!"

"See you, Dad!"

"Who was that?" Joe asked as she came back into the room, turned the record over, and resumed her position on the bed.

"Just my father."

"Doesn't he live with you?"

"He left when I was two. We don't see much of him. He rings up when he's feeling guilty. We never have much to say."

"Unlike you and me."

"Very unlike you and me."

They kissed again. Soon, thoughts about her father and his mythical holidays were a million miles away. Lorna knocked the novel she was reading down the side of the bed, but didn't even notice. All she could think about was the sensation of Joe's warm body pressing against hers. It was the best feeling she'd ever known.

Chapter 9

"**Y**ou turned down a holiday in California! What were you thinking of?"

"I didn't turn it down, not exactly."

"I can still go, can't I?" Ben asked.

"You know what Dad's like," Lorna told him, "always promising things and not delivering."

"Yes, but he's never mentioned firm dates before," Mum insisted. "Your father's a workaholic, always has been. Spending more than a weekend away from rows of figures turns him into a quivering wreck."

Lorna didn't argue with this. Mum went on.

"It sounds to me like he's finally worked out a way to fit two children around work for a few weeks. You have to go, Lorna. Apart from anything else, you'll really need a holiday after your exams, and I can't afford to give you one."

Lorna shrugged. She wasn't going to say anything about Joe.

"I can still go, can't I, even if Lorna won't?" Ben asked again.

"If your father means it, I expect so," Mum said. "Did he say when he'd ring again?"

"He wants Joe to write him a letter, with end-of-term dates and all that."

"*Joe*? Who's Joe?"

Lorna tightened up inside, realizing her mistake.

"I mean Ben."

Before Mum could question her further, Ben began asking for pen and paper, so that he could write to his father immediately. While Mum was digging in a cupboard for the end-of-term dates, Lorna beat a hasty retreat.

At school the next day, Lorna sat with Sulvinder in the form room. Abby and Melissa arrived and began talking about a film they'd been to the night before. It was funny — Abby had been round to Lorna's house yesterday, but she hadn't suggested the film to her. Sometimes, these days, those two operated like an exclusive club.

"Hey, Lorna!"

It was Kristi Smythe, one of the louder girls in the form.

"Is it true about you and Joe?"

"Joe who?"

Kristi turned back to Carmel Carter.

"Told you!"

Mel and Abby showed no sign of having heard the exchange.

"Are you going to tell them?" Sulvinder asked.

"I suppose I'll have to," Lorna said. "I wasn't going to say anything until I was sure we were serious."

"But, after yesterday afternoon . . ." Sulvinder prompted.

"After yesterday afternoon, I'm sure we are."

Later, they walked past the sixth form centre. Jazz waved at both of them.

"I'm thinking of staying here to go to the sixth form," Sulvinder said.

"Don't," Lorna insisted. "It's full of the same old boring people. We need to go somewhere new. There are lots more courses at the Sixth Form college."

"Maybe," Sulvinder said.

"You're not thinking of changing your plans just because of a boy?" Lorna asked, with a slight sneer in her voice.

"Maybe," Sulvinder said. "What's Joe doing next year, anyway?"

"I haven't asked him yet."

But Lorna did ask him, in English. They were waiting outside the classroom and no one else had arrived. Yesterday, they'd agreed to remain aloof in school — that was what people did, if they were going out with each other: anything else was considered decidedly uncool — but once they were together, it was hard to resist a small hug.

"What are you doing next year?" Lorna asked, in a whisper. "Are you staying in this dump?"

Joe shook his head.

"I put my college application in back in January," he said. Lorna sighed with relief. Miss Tate opened the door.

"If you two stand any closer together," she said, giving them a funny look, "people'll think you're about to take part in a three-legged race."

They walked in and sat, as usual, at opposite ends of the room.

Lorna was glad that English was the only lesson she shared with Joe. For the first time ever, she felt tongue-tied this morning. When Miss Tate asked her a question, she clammed up, and was only able to mumble an inadequate answer. Sulvinder filled in for her. Joe, too, she noticed, failed to come up with his usual witticisms.

"When can I see you again?" he asked, sliding past her at the end of the lesson.

"Abby and Melissa were on about this film they went to see. Do you like going to the pictures? We could . . ."

"How about tonight?"

Lorna beamed at him. Joe hadn't even bothered to ask what film they were going to see.

"Fine," she said. "I'll find out when the showing starts and give you a ring."

"OK."

He squeezed her waist before walking off.

"You two don't waste any time," Sulvinder said, as they headed off towards Media Studies.

Today, Abby was making some last-minute alterations to her credit sequence on the video editing machine. Brian Kane was hanging round her, anxious to get on with his film. Most of the other students were spread round the school, photocopying, researching, or skiving off. Even Mrs

Wright, their teacher, had "just popped out" to the staffroom, where she was doubtless having a cup of coffee and a good gossip. Lorna, Melissa and Sulvinder chatted. They had finished all their work. So, for them, the course was over, even though they had to keep going to lessons until May.

"I heard a rumour about you today," Melissa said, lowering her heavy glasses slightly so that they gave her a slightly comic look.

"About me?" Lorna said.

"You should have heard Abby tearing into Simon Pinto," Mel told her. "She made him look really silly. You know what he said?" Lorna and Sulvinder looked at each other.

"You'd better tell her," Sulvinder said.

Lorna agreed. She wanted to get it over with.

"I bet she said I was going out with Joe Green."

"That's right," Melissa said. "You heard too. Who started it?"

"No one started it," Lorna said, feeling her face go red. "You see, it's not a rumour. It's true."

Melissa blinked. Then she stood up.

"Abby!" she called. "Come over here."

Abby looked up from the RME-300.

"I'll only be a moment."

Abby was rewinding her tape. Brian Kane leant forward and his long hair brushed her shoulder.

"I'm nearly through," Abby said. "Thanks for being patient." She pulled out the tape and walked over to the three girls.

"What's so urgent?"

Melissa gave a smug smile. She obviously loved having the news first.

"Lorna's got something to tell you."

Abby smiled. She had perfect, pearly-white teeth. No one would have argued if you had described her as being beautiful. However, right now, Lorna thought she looked like a vulture, about to pounce.

"Don't tell me," Abby said, in a supercilious voice. "The rumours about you and Joe Green are true."

Lorna was surprised.

"How did you know?" she asked.

Abby's face fell. For once, Lorna really had caught her unawares.

"I don't . . . no! You and Joe? Come on, Lorna, you're winding me up. Aren't you?"

Slowly, Lorna shook her head. She had never seen Abby at such a loss for words before.

"How . . . how could you?" she spluttered out. "He's so . . . infantile!"

Lorna hoped Sulvinder or Melissa would defend Joe. But they didn't.

"You don't really know him," she told Abby, "or you wouldn't say that."

Now Abby's eyes were blazing.

"Don't you remember all those conversations we had?" she asked, mockingly. "About what jerks the boys around here are, about waiting until the exams are over and then maybe dating older boys? Didn't you mean all of that?"

"Of course I *meant* it!" Lorna insisted. "But things happen. You can't turn your back on them. My going out with Joe isn't going to stop me seeing my friends, or doing well in my exams."

"Isn't it?" Abby asked. "Take a look around you. Half the girls in our year have discovered sex and aren't bothered about schoolwork any more. Their hormones rule their heads."

"You're being unfair," Lorna said.

"To them, or to you? Get a life, Lorna! I don't know what's got into you, throwing yourself away on somebody like Joe."

Now Lorna began to lose her temper.

"You're the one who should get a life! Always looking down on people all the time because they don't make top grades or watch Channel 4 News. Maybe you'll make it, Abby. Maybe some movie star'll come along and sweep you up. But we're not all as good looking as you. We can't all afford to turn down every boy who finds us attractive."

Abby looked affronted.

"So you go out with the first boy who shows the least bit of interest in you?"

"Who says he's the first?"

"Who else then?"

Lorna thought about the Valentine she had been sent. She hadn't told Abby about it. Maybe the card was from Joe. Maybe it wasn't. But she wasn't going to mention that now, so she kept silent. Abby looked triumphant.

"So you're going out with a boy you couldn't stand a week ago. Fine. I wish you well. But I warn you, Lorna, he won't be any good for you. Sooner or later, he'll mess you about. Boys like him always do."

"How would you know?"

Both of them were really raising their voices now.

"I know because the only place you'll find a boy good enough for you is in one of those ancient novels you're always slipping into the bottom of your bag, Lorna Haines. That's how I know."

"Hey! Girls, girls."

Brian Kane had come over from the editing machine.

"I can't concentrate when you're shouting like that."

Abby stared daggers at him. Lorna felt embarrassed.

"Also . . ." He pointed out of the window. "Look who's coming." Mrs Wright was returning to the room.

"Thanks, Brian," Lorna said, and got out an essay she had to finish for Geography.

"I knew she'd take it badly," Sulvinder said. "But I didn't think she'd take it that badly."

Lorna was silent. She felt like crying.

"She didn't get to you, did she?" Sulvinder asked.

"Of course not," Lorna replied.

But it wasn't true. Part of Lorna suspected that Abby had it right. She was setting herself up for a fall. But that was mad. She was going out with Joe tonight. Abby was jealous, that was all.

Mrs Wright came in and immediately insisted on looking at Abby's finished video. Normally, Lorna and Sulvinder would have gone over with Melissa and looked at it too. But today they stayed in their corner of the room. For the rest of the lesson they worked in silence, not acknowledging that a friendship which had dominated Lorna's life for ten-and-a-half years seemed to be about to break up. Lorna could do without Abby, after all. She still had Sulvinder. And, even more importantly, she had Joe.

Chapter 10

"What's this film about then?" Joe asked as they bought their tickets.

"I don't know. Abby and Mel said it was really good."

As soon as Lorna said this, she knew she'd made a mistake. Joe wrinkled his nose as though he was sniffing.

"Oh. Well, I'll try not to hold that against it."

They walked into the Savoy. It was the oldest cinema in town and was commonly referred to as the "flea-pit". However, it had one great advantage over the other cinemas which Lorna had forgotten until now.

"Hey, we'll have to sit in one of those," Joe said.

"Those" were double seats, with no divide down the middle, where couples could cuddle all the way through the film. There was one on each row.

"They're called 'love seats'," Joe told her.

"And how many girls have you shared one of these seats with before?" Lorna asked him, jokingly. The tone of her voice concealed how serious the question was to her.

"None," Joe insisted, as though he'd been accused of a crime. "You're the first girl I've taken out. In fact, you're the first girl I've even asked out, ever."

Lorna smiled. She'd hoped this would be so. They kissed — a long, passionate kiss which lasted until the adverts started. The feel of his warm body pressing against hers was wonderful.

"I can't believe these commercials," Joe said. "Whenever I go to the pictures they have the same ones: the girl making the coffee in the car and deciding not to kill herself, the hip white guy going out with the gorgeous black girl and drinking Southern Comfort. Do you think that they've been showing these ads since before we were born?"

"Probably," Lorna said.

They had to sit through fifteen minutes of adverts and trailers before the film began, but it didn't matter. Joe provided a running commentary on the inadequacies of whatever they were watching. When he wasn't making Lorna laugh, he was kissing her.

Then the film began. It was subtitled, which Lorna hadn't realized. She had to put her glasses back on. They stopped kissing, but Joe put his arm around her, and they sat so close together that Lorna felt a kind of thrill whenever Joe shuffled slightly in his seat.

He did this quite a lot as the film went on. It was the story of a young girl, Eloïse, in rural France in the eighteenth century. She was brought up by a solitary farmer who she thought was her father. The father kept Eloïse away from other people, educating her a little himself. However, by the age of fifteen, Eloïse had become very beautiful and independent, and began to venture further afield while her father was in the fields during the day.

All this took about half an hour to establish, and Joe was clearly getting bored. Lorna was enjoying the film, but wished they'd gone to see something more fast-moving instead. This was beautiful to look at, and she identified with the girl, but Joe clearly didn't.

Next, Eloïse met a much older man, and they fell in love with each other. The father nearly interrupted them as they were making love in a barn. Just as the girl discovered that she was pregnant, the film stopped. The words "Intermission" appeared on the screen.

"I'd forgotten they did that," Lorna said. "This is the only cinema where they still have an interval."

"Well, I'm glad," Joe told her. "I need a drink after an hour of that. Any decent soap opera would have conveyed the storyline in less than ten minutes."

He bought her a drink in the small bar.

"Are you enjoying it?" he asked her.

"Yes. But I'd be enjoying it more if you were too."

Joe shrugged.

"They're all the same, those French films. They all have that Depardieu bloke in them and they're always full of people who don't say much and

incredible coincidences. I had to watch a couple
of them on TV over Christmas. They're so predictable."

"I suppose you can tell me what's going to
happen in the rest of this one," Lorna teased him.

"I wouldn't want to spoil it for you."

Lorna punched him playfully.

"You don't really know what's going to happen."

Joe shrugged.

"Not precisely, no. But I'll bet the bloke she just
had sex with is really her father and when
Depardieu, who's her grandad, finds out, one of
them'll kill the other."

Lorna laughed.

"That's preposterous. But it's good. You ought to
write films yourself."

"They couldn't be worse than that one," Joe told
her.

Lorna decided to make a sacrifice.

"We don't have to go back in if you don't want to.
We could stay up here till it's time to go."

"No," Joe said, "you're all right. We may as well
see if I've got it right."

They kissed again as a middle-aged voice over
the tannoy informed them that the film was about
to resume.

The story was a little more complicated than
Joe had guessed, but he'd worked out the basics:
when the father met the girl's lover, he recognized
him and went crazy. There was a fight in which
the father was killed. The lover then realized that
he had fallen for the daughter he never knew he
had, fathered shortly before he went off to fight in

a war. Eloïse explained that her mother had died in childbirth. This news drove her lover/father mad, and he tried to kill himself but failed, ending up half paralyzed.

The daughter found herself looking after both her real father, now bedridden, and their incestuous child. The ending was very sad and creepy, but it had taken a long time coming and Joe was obviously very bored. As soon as the closing credits came up, they got up to go.

"Now for the bit I'm really dreading," Joe said, grimly.

Lorna had arranged for her mum to pick them both up and give Joe a lift home. She'd managed to avoid telling Mum who Joe was, simply mentioning a "friend" from Coddington who Mum hadn't met before. But Mum wasn't stupid. She'd soon work out what kind of a friend Joe was.

The red Astra was already waiting when they walked out of the cinema, hand in hand. There was a slight chill in the breeze. Lorna put on a forced smile as she watched Mum unlock the back doors of the car. Joe, being gallant, opened the door for her, then walked round to the other side and got in.

"This is Joe," Lorna said, as they did up their seat belts.

"Hello, Joe."

Joe replied brightly and Mum started to drive.

"Good film?"

"It was all right," Lorna said.

"Do you think I'd enjoy it?"

"Probably. It was a bit slow."

"Oh, I like slow films," Mum said in a jovial tone. "Most things are far too quick for me. My brain's slowing down. It must be old age."

Lorna felt acutely embarrassed. Why did Mum need to witter on like this?

"What did you think of the film, Joe?"

"Not a lot. It was a bit predictable. I'm not too keen on films with subtitles."

"Mmm."

Lorna wished he hadn't made that last comment. Mum and Ric were both film buffs. One of their pet hates was foreign films where English voices were dubbed onto the soundtrack. They insisted on films being left in the original language with subtitles added.

"Whereabouts do you live, Joe?"

Joe told her. Mum began to pump him for information about what his parents did and how many brothers and sisters he had. Lorna cringed. She hadn't asked Joe any questions like that herself. The answers weren't important.

They pulled up outside Joe's house, a non-descript semi much like Lorna's own.

"I'll see you tomorrow," Joe said. He kissed her chastely on the cheek, but his hand squeezed the top of her thigh, sending sweet shivers through her body.

"Sorry you didn't like the film," she repeated. "Next time, you choose."

"I'll hold you to that. G'night."

Mum drove off. For two minutes she didn't say a word, and neither did Lorna. Lorna wondered who would be the first to crack before they got home.

Streets passed in silence and Lorna began to relax. Her life had changed over the last three days. She felt that she was living in a new, friendlier world, where only good things could happen.

Finally, it was Mum who spoke.

"He seems like a nice boy," she said.

"Did you think so?" Lorna replied, noncommitally.

"I suppose you're going to tell me you're just good friends."

"I wasn't planning on telling you anything."

Mum laughed awkwardly.

"I thought we were closer than that. I also remember you telling me, on your sixteenth birthday, that you weren't going to have any boyfriends until you'd finished your exams."

"Maybe that was because I thought no one would ask me," Lorna replied, more honestly than she'd intended.

"Aaah," Mum said, as she parked outside the house.

Lorna went upstairs as soon as she got in, and put on the k d lang record that she'd enjoyed with Joe the previous afternoon. Every track on it was a love song, and she identified with every word of each one. Joe had been so nice to her tonight, even though he hadn't enjoyed the film. Lorna couldn't wait until the morning so that she could see him again. As the final chorus of *Constant Craving* died out, she slipped off into dreams of a perfect love, true and everlasting, softer and warmer than anything she'd ever known.

Chapter 11

The next day the mock results came out. Instead of the teachers giving them to you in lessons, as had happened with previous exams, the school gave you a report, which had the grades in one corner, your class position in another, and a teacher comment underneath. All but one of Lorna's grades was an "A".

The teacher comments were especially excessive: "An ideal student"; "She can succeed in any area she puts her mind to"; "Bound to do exceedingly well in whatever area she chooses in the sixth form", her tutor had written. They were trying to soften her up into staying at Westtown Comp. They had no chance.

Lorna bumped into Joe at lunch. He smiled bashfully and asked about her report.

"It was OK."

"Show me."

Lorna refused to get the report out.

"It's embarrassing."

"You can see mine if you want."

Lorna shook her head.

"I don't."

Joe shrugged.

"I expect you're being wise. But it's not a bad one. I'm in the middle for practically everything. Nice, safe place to be, the middle. People leave you alone there."

Lorna laughed.

"People who stand in the middle of the road are liable to get knocked over," she quoted at him.

Joe grinned.

"Who said that? No, let me guess. Groucho Marx?"

Lorna shook her head.

"Oscar Wilde?"

Lorna shook her head again.

"Margaret Thatcher," she said.

"Thatcher? What are you doing quoting someone like her? I thought you told me your mum was in the Labour party?"

"That's my mum, not me. Anyway, I didn't say I agreed with her. As far as I'm concerned, you can stay in the middle of the road, as long as I can pick you up whenever I'm passing."

"It's a deal."

They laughed, and, since no one was around in the common room, kissed. Lorna felt on top of the world. The report in her pocket meant nothing to her. Joe's love was everything.

"Hi!" Joe mumbled as they broke away from each other.

Lorna turned round to see who Joe was greeting.

It was Melissa and Abby. The atmosphere in the room went cold.

"Hi," Lorna said, too.

Abby nodded. Melissa started to smile, then stopped.

"We went to see that film you recommended last night," she told Abby.

Abby couldn't quite bring herself to ignore Lorna.

"Did you?"

"Interesting film," Joe said, making an effort to be friendly.

"I thought the tracking shots were really unimaginative," Abby pronounced, "and the flashback towards the end was clumsy."

"What flashback?" Joe asked.

Lorna felt embarrassed. Why did Abby always have to show off? She picked up the conversation.

"The ending was depressing, though, wasn't it?"

"I thought it was deeply ironic," Abby said, in a tone which implied that Joe, at least, wouldn't know what she was talking about.

"I'm not sure I agree," Lorna said. "Don't you think that 'irony' is a really over-used word?"

Abby glared at her.

"No," she said. "I don't. I think 'interesting' is a really over-used word. And so is 'love'. They're both used a lot by people who don't really mean them."

"What's her problem?" Joe asked, when they'd gone.

"I'm not entirely sure," Lorna said.

They sat down. She tried to explain.

"It's partly because the four of us — me, Sulvinder, Melissa and Abby — agreed not to have boyfriends until our exams were over."

Joe seemed surprised.

"What?"

"I know it sounds silly now, but there were sensible reasons at the time. Abby's not that keen on boys. It's made worse by the fact that boys are always pestering her to go out with them and she's just not interested. They get on her nerves."

Joe shook his head.

"You wouldn't catch me pestering her for a date."

"I'd better not!" Lorna punched him in the stomach. "Or I'll beat you up."

The subject of Abby was closed.

It seemed that everything in Lorna's life had become much lighter since she'd started going out with Joe. She still got all of her school work done, but spent less time on it. She didn't have to be a perfectionist about everything — that was one thing she'd learnt from Joe. Over the next month, she saw him three or four evenings a week. Not all evening, unless they went to a film or a party, but they usually managed to snatch an hour in one of their bedrooms, halfway to heaven in each other's arms. They were both cautious, neither of them saying the words for what they were feeling. But the feeling was there.

Lorna got on well with Joe's family. She had dinner there twice. Joe had a brother of Ben's age and a sister two years younger. Lorna treated the brother much better than she treated Ben, pretending an interest in computer games purely for the sake of conversation. Then she listened to the sister's endless monologues about her favourite horse books with a convincing show of interest. Joe told Lorna she'd made a big hit with his parents.

"They even credit you with making me work harder at school."

"Are you?"

Joe gave his pouting little smile.

"No. But I tell them I am."

After a month, Lorna could no longer avoid inviting Joe round for a meal with Mum, Ben and Ric. She wanted to exclude Ric, but Mum insisted.

"He's practically family."

"Does that mean you're getting married?"

"No, it doesn't," Mum told her, with a wry smile. "The arrangement as it stands suits me very well. I don't want a man around the house all the time. They lose their charm."

But the evening wasn't a success. Ric and Joe were similar in some ways, Lorna decided — always making a joke out of everything and using flattery to get what they wanted. But Ric, with all his experience, overshadowed Joe. Worse, he kept asking Joe questions — about school, music, films and books — which Joe would normally have had fun with. Tonight, though, he found them hard to answer.

Joe and Lorna did the washing up while Mum and Ric went out. Ben was staying overnight at a friend's house, so for once they had the house to themselves. Upstairs in Lorna's bedroom, Joe was apologetic about his lack of conversation earlier.

"I felt a bit out of my depth. I mean, your mum's a university lecturer, and that bloke teaches at the Sixth Form college. I didn't want to show myself up."

Lorna smiled sympathetically.

"It doesn't matter."

"You mean I'm allowed to love you without loving your whole family and assorted hangers-on too?"

Lorna felt her heart beat more quickly.

"What did you say?"

"I said, 'So I don't have to love your whole . . .'"

"Before that . . ."

Joe grinned impishly.

"It wasn't a big deal. All I was trying to say was 'I love you'."

Lorna could feel her heart melting.

"You've never said that before."

"I know. But I have now."

"I love you too," Lorna whispered.

They embraced. Lorna was his now, utterly and completely in love. Tonight was their night and she would remember it for the rest of her life. Whatever happened next, neither of them would regret it. The knowledge of their love was delicious. Better than waking up on Christmas morning with a pile of presents at the bottom of the bed. Better than the ideal of love in the Victorian novels she read. Better. Better. Best.

Chapter 12

"What was it like?" Sulvinder asked, in a low, fascinated voice, as they sat at the lunch table.

Lorna shook her head.

"It was like . . . oh, I'm sorry. I can't . . . it was really exciting. It all happened so quickly. It was kind of weird, like I knew it was happening to me but I'd become someone else. No, that's not right either. We were careful, but neither of us had really planned it. I guess I just didn't have time to think how I'd describe it afterwards."

Sulvinder smiled. It must make a change for her to see Lorna at a loss for words, yet still managing to come out with so many.

"Are you glad you did it?" she asked Lorna, gently.

Lorna thought for a moment.

"It's so weird. When Mum came home and said goodnight to Joe, I was sure she could tell — like we were wearing badges or something. But she didn't say anything. I mean . . . I'm sure she'd say we should have waited. What do you think?"

Sulvinder frowned slightly.

"I would have waited. But I'm not you. I wouldn't do it until I'm engaged, at least. It wouldn't feel right."

"But what if Jazz tried to persuade you? What if he made you feel right?"

Sulvinder gave an embarrassed shrug.

"Jazz wouldn't act that way. Not with me. He'd show more respect."

"Why do you say 'not with me'?" Lorna asked.

Sulvinder shrugged.

"You know how it is. Sikhs have double standards, the same as everybody else. Girls can't sleep around. But some of the boys have white girlfriends, and no one makes much of it, unless they marry them."

"But Jazz's father's white!"

Sulvinder nodded.

"Standards are different for men and women — a Sikh woman going out with a white man would get all kinds of grief. I think that the community froze Jazz's mother out. When they got married, none of her family came to the wedding. Jazz says that the first two years of the marriage were very rough. But people have become a lot more tolerant in the last few years, and Jazz's father is very successful, which must help. So they're accepted now."

"How does Jazz feel about all that?" Lorna asked.

Sulvinder thought for a moment.

"Colour doesn't make much difference to him, but he is religious. Not in the same way as my family, though. His are much more liberated."

"Don't you mean 'liberal'?" Lorna asked.

"No," Sulvinder said. "I don't."

As they were about to get up to go, Abby came over and sat down next to them.

"I haven't seen much of you two recently."

Lorna felt guilty. She and Sulvinder had been spending most of their free time with their boyfriends. But Abby, despite her hang-ups and occasional arrogance, was still Lorna's oldest friend.

"I'm sorry," Sulvinder said. "We've been . . . uh . . ."

"Don't apologize," Abby told her, cheerfully. "I just wanted to tell you that my mum's letting me have a party for my sixteenth, the Saturday before we go back to school after Easter. So of course you're invited, with a friend each."

Lorna was surprised. Abby smiled and suddenly looked very sincere.

"I know I've been a bit tetchy the last few weeks," she told the two girls. "I'm sorry. It's my problem, not yours. I'd hate us to stop being friends."

"So would we," Lorna said, meaning it.

"That's right," Sulvinder said.

Abby went off. Lorna and Sulvinder looked at each other.

"Abby having a party!" Sulvinder said.

"What's got into her?" Lorna asked. "I hope I can persuade Joe to go. He can't stand her."

"After last night," Sulvinder said, "I'm sure you can persuade him to do anything."

That night, in his bedroom, Joe wasn't very keen.

"Who else will she have invited?" he wanted to know.

Lorna shrugged.

"Does it matter? We'll both be there and you know Sulvinder."

Actually, Joe didn't find it easy to talk to Sulvinder. They had little in common, apart from Lorna. And he wasn't very friendly with Jazz either, despite having been invited to his party. It wasn't their different racial backgrounds which separated them, but their ages. Girls could be friendly with boys a year older than them. Boys couldn't.

"Look," she told Joe, "I know you don't like Abby much, and she can be really . . . superior at times, but she has a nice, warm side, too. And I've been friends with her since primary school. So please try."

"Why?" Joe wanted to know. "I mean, why have you been friends with her all this time when you know how self-centred she can be?"

"It's difficult to explain," Lorna said. "Do people really choose their friends? I don't know."

"You're always doing that," Joe told her.

"Doing what?"

"I ask you a specific question and you turn it into a what-do-you-call-it? An abstraction. Like you're showing off. Maybe that's what you have in common with Abigail Thomas."

Lorna began to sulk.

"Why are you being like this? It isn't like you."

Joe looked apologetic and cuddled her.

"I'm sorry. She just rubs me up the wrong way."

"I know. But come to the party, for me."

"Of course I will."

They had nearly had an argument, but it seemed to have brought them closer. Joe began to whisper sweet things into her ear. He kissed her so softly, yet held her so tightly. His arms were firm yet gentle at the same time. Their bodies melted into each other. Lorna felt a sense of amazement. This was what being in love was about, and, somehow, it kept getting better, all the time.

A week later, Miss Tate handed back Lorna's essay on the role of the rude mechanicals in *A Midsummer-Night's Dream* with a reproachful look. She asked Lorna to see her at the end of the lesson. Lorna glanced quickly at the end of the essay. Her grade had dropped from the usual "A" to a "B".

"I hope that was only a temporary slip, Lorna," Miss Tate said later. "This wasn't up to your normal standard at all. It was thin on quotation. The conclusion was sloppy and you even made several spelling mistakes. You hadn't drafted it, had you?"

Lorna shrugged apologetically.

"I can't be perfect all the time."

Lorna wasn't usually cheeky to teachers. She surprised herself. Miss Tate looked disappointed.

"You don't know how often I've seen this before, Lorna. I hate it when it happens to girls like you. School's going brilliantly, then you start dating a boy, discover sex and everything goes to pot. It's Joe Green, isn't it?"

"I don't see what . . ."

Lorna had always got on well with Miss Tate, but didn't see how this gave the teacher the right to comment on her private life. Before she could finish, Miss Tate interrupted.

"He's a nice lad, though you make a surprising couple. Try not to let him mess up your exam chances, Lorna. I know he doesn't work as hard as you do. Don't let him pull you down to his level."

"That's not fair," Lorna said. "What right have you got to butt into my private life? The exams aren't for two more months, and how I do in them is my business, no one else's."

"You know that's not true," Miss Tate told her patiently. "You're an especially gifted girl, who could go very far indeed. I suspect that all of your teachers put in extra work to make sure we're stretching you."

She paused, and folded her arms. Lorna decided not to interrupt her.

"Of course, if you get good marks, we get some credit, too. But not that much. You owe it to everyone, not just yourself, to do well."

"What was all that about?" Joe asked, as they had lunch together. "I've never known you to be kept behind before."

"It was nothing," Lorna lied. "I wanted some advice on where I went wrong in my essay."

"You went wrong?" Joe's voice was incredulous. "What mark did you get?"

"A 'B'."

"A 'B'? You call that going wrong? The best mark I've had all year is a 'C+'."

Lorna changed the subject quickly, before she could put her foot in it again.

Chapter 13

The night before Abby's party, Lorna's father rang.

"He wants to talk to you," Mum called up the stairs, getting Lorna out of bed. "He's muddled up the time zones again."

Dad's voice boomed down the phone. The longer he was away, the stronger his American accent became.

"Hi, sweetheart! No loud music tonight? No boyfriend?"

"I don't see him every night. Anyway, it's nearly midnight. I was asleep."

Dad didn't apologize.

"I'm ringing about the holiday. I've got all the dates sorted out. Last week of July till the third week of August in the golden state. How are you fixed?"

"Well . . ."

"Your mother tells me you want to bring your boyfriend along."

"Yes," said Lorna, relieved that she didn't have to explain herself.

"Your mum thinks I should let you, but I'm not sure. Tell me, how does he get on with Ben?"

"Fine."

This wasn't strictly true. Ben and Joe hardly had any contact. Dad ummed and aahed.

"Please," she said, in a breathy, begging voice.

Dad relented.

"I tell you what – if his parents can come up with the air fare and some pocket money, I'll stand the motel rooms and meal bills while he's over here. How's that?"

"It sounds really generous, Dad, though I don't know if . . ."

"Yeah, well, the exchange rate's in our favour at the moment. Anyway, it shouldn't cost too much. He can share a room with your brother."

Lorna felt a great burst of happiness.

"It'll be good to see you again, Dad. It's been too long."

"Same feeling here. But don't let your boyfriend dither. Flights can be murder to get in the holiday season. I need a decision by next weekend. All right?"

"All right."

Lorna went back to bed, wishing she could call Joe now. It was an exciting prospect – four weeks in California with Joe at her side. She was sure he'd jump at it.

Joe and Lorna had seen each other every day of the two-week Easter holiday. They were supposed to be revising together, but somehow very little work got done. On Saturday evening, she told him about her father's holiday proposal. He didn't seem as excited as she was.

"I don't know," Joe said, as they walked to the party hand in hand. "Four weeks. I'm not sure my mum and dad would wear it."

"Why not?" Lorna replied. "I'm sure they wouldn't mind having you off their hands."

"I think they've already booked a fortnight in Jersey."

Lorna was hurt.

"Jersey? Why didn't you mention it before?"

"Why didn't you mention California before?" Joe replied. "You just said that you've known about it for over a month."

"I told you – my dad's always making these promises that he never gets round to keeping."

"So how do you know he's going to keep this one?" Joe retorted.

"Because I do," Lorna insisted. "Look, don't be like this, Joe. Ask your parents, please."

"I'll ask. But the flight on its own could be a lot of money. We'd have to pay the full adult fare, you know."

"I know."

Lorna left it at that. It hadn't occurred to her that Joe's family wouldn't be able to afford the air fare. Maybe, even if they wouldn't let Joe go, the Greens could take Lorna on holiday with them instead. She wouldn't mind if she had to share a room with Joe's younger sister. Suddenly, it seemed very important to Lorna that she should go away somewhere, anywhere, with Joe this summer.

Chapter 14

Abby's party was a low-key affair. There was more talking than dancing and Joe looked bored. Some couples were smooching in corners, but Joe and Lorna were past that stage now. Lorna found it very hard not to touch him all the time. She could see other girls at the party looking at him admiringly, which made her feel very proud.

"You look so happy all the time," Melissa told her. "I'm really pleased for you."

"Thanks," Lorna said. "Tell me, are you and Abby still keeping to the pact we all made at the beginning of the year?"

"No boyfriends? There's not much choice where I'm concerned. No one ever asks me out. It's Abby they're after. My only chance of a bloke would be as the short straw in a double date."

"That's not true," Lorna said. "You could easily . . ."

Melissa shook her head resignedly.

"No, I couldn't."

Lorna wasn't really sure if the stuff about boys not asking Mel out was true or not. Melissa and Abby were always trying to outdo each other in the cynicism stakes.

The doorbell rang, and, since she was nearest the door, Lorna went to answer it. Jazz and Sulvinder stood there. He was wearing brown jeans and a black linen Paul Smith shirt. Lorna recognized it from the shop window. Sulvinder wore jeans and a bright "Greenpeace" T-shirt.

"Arriving together?" Lorna teased them. "People will talk."

"Let them," Jazz said, but Sulvinder shushed him with a smile.

Abby greeted Sulvinder breezily. Then she saw Jazz. Her expression changed. She looked from Jazz to Sulvinder and back again. Lorna guessed that she had only just registered that Sulvinder was actually going out with Jazz. It would be a shock to Abby. First Lorna, now Sulvinder.

"Glad you could come," Abby muttered to Jazz.

Lorna felt like dancing. She went over to Abby, who was talking to Jazz's sister, and suggested turning the music up.

"OK," Abby said. "But I'd better start it. I guess that means I have to find someone to dance with."

Lorna looked around. Suggesting a partner for Abby was a complex decision. Some of the boys here would jump through hoops for her at the slightest sign of encouragement.

Tonight, Abby looked stunning. Her long hair

was brushed back and she wore a simple, backless white dress which showed all her curves to full advantage. Sometimes there was a hardness to her face which made her less attractive, but tonight she looked surprisingly vulnerable. It was the first party Lorna could remember her having since she was ten years old.

But who would dance with her? Typically, Abby hadn't invited a boy for herself. Lorna thought of asking Joe to partner her. But they didn't get on, and anyway, Lorna wanted to dance with Joe herself. If she saw Abby in his arms, she knew she would feel jealous.

Then Jazz saw the situation. He walked over to Abby, leaving Sulvinder as though she were a mere casual acquaintance – which, as far as most people were concerned, she was.

"May I have this dance?" he asked, acting like a matinee idol. Abby smiled eagerly.

A reggae song came on and Lorna turned the volume up. Joe joined her. She felt as if she was in heaven, dancing joyfully with him in the middle of the room. Beside them, Abby and Jazz made a handsome couple. Several boys gave the tall, attractive youth envious looks. Soon the room was full of people dancing. Abby quickly returned to the conversational group in the other room, allowing Jazz to dance with Sulvinder.

Sulvinder, too, seemed to be finding it hard to conceal her happiness. This is a golden time, Lorna thought, as Joe held her in his strong arms during a slow song. I want it to last forever.

*　　*　　*

But this party didn't go on as long as Jazz's had. People started leaving soon after eleven. Sulvinder had to go at half past, despite Lorna urging her to stay.

"If I don't make my curfew tonight, Mum and Dad won't let me go to another party in a hurry."

"Do you want me to come with you?"

"No. It's OK."

Sulvinder glanced over Lorna's shoulder. Lorna turned round to see Jazz putting on his leather jacket.

"He's going to walk me home and then come back to the party," Sulvinder smiled shyly.

"But he's not *really* your boyfriend," Lorna teased.

"He's escorting me home because he's a gentleman," she said. "At least that's what I'll say to my parents if anyone tells them about it."

Lorna watched the couple leave from the hallway. As they turned the corner, she thought she saw Sulvinder slipping her hand into Jazz's.

Jazz returned half an hour later. In the interim, the dancing had stopped. The remaining dozen people sat around in the lounge, drinking coffee and holding desultory conversations about music, books and green issues. It was the kind of conversation Lorna liked. Although she was often withdrawn in company, she found herself chipping in now and then. Joe, however, looked bored.

"Shall we go?" he asked, as Jazz began to talk about the way in which racism still permeated every level of society.

"Wait a bit," Lorna said. "I'm really interested in this." She was about to ask Jazz a question when Joe stood up.

"I'm afraid I'll have to make a move," he told Abby. "Thanks for the great party."

"It was nice of you to come," Abby said graciously.

Lorna got up too. She wasn't tired, but she couldn't stay and have Joe leave without her.

"Are you walking?" Jazz asked. "Because I'll be driving home in a while, if you want a lift."

Jazz had passed his driving test the previous month.

"No, really," Joe told him. "We'll be fine."

It was a three-quarter-hour walk to Joe's house, and the night had turned cool. Lorna wondered why Joe had turned down the lift. She asked him if he wanted to stop at her house for a coffee before walking home. He turned her down.

"No. I'm tired. I'd better get going."

Lorna frowned.

"If you're tired, why didn't you hang around for a bit and accept Jazz's offer of a lift? It's not as though he's been drinking or anything. He's a good driver."

Joe shook his head.

"I dunno . . ." he mumbled. "I find it hard to make conversation with guys like him. I mean, I know the stuff about racism's important, but I don't know much about it, you know."

"You didn't have to talk to him in the car."

"Yeah. But if I don't have anything to say it makes me look like a jerk, doesn't it?"

Lorna stroked his face.

"You're not a jerk."

Joe shrugged.

"You thought I was one once."

He kissed her.

"I wish you'd come in," she said. "Just for a while."

Joe shook his head.

"I feel like walking," he told her, "on my own, having a think about things."

"OK," Lorna told him. "Sometimes I feel that way too."

"I'll call you tomorrow."

"Fine."

They kissed again, more softly than before, and didn't break away for a long time.

"Don't forget to ask your parents about America," Lorna called, as he walked off towards the village.

"I won't."

Lorna went upstairs to bed, but found it hard to close her eyes. Her head was filled with fantasies of open-topped sports cars, and ocean breeze, and Joe by her side. This year, it seemed, all of her dreams were coming true. Why not one more? She looked at the pile of unopened school books on her desk, but her eyes didn't focus on them at all. All she could see was Joe.

Chapter 15

School started again and Lorna became aware of the torrent of work she hadn't done over the holidays. There was a month to go before the fifth form went on study leave. At the beginning of the year, Lorna had promised herself that she would do three hours' revision a day during the holiday. As it turned out, she hadn't even kept up with her homework. Still, as Joe kept reminding her, she was so far ahead of most of the people in her year that she could afford to relax now and then.

Joe, too, was well behind in his work, so they didn't see each other in the evenings as often as they had been doing. Lorna was anxious to get the California trip sorted out. However, every time she brought it up, Joe hadn't asked his parents.

"I've got to choose the right moment," he explained. "It's not as easy as all that."

Lorna didn't like to pressure him, so she left it. School wasn't the best place to talk about things like that, anyway.

Then Dad phoned up again, and the decision became more urgent.

"Flight availability is extremely limited, sweetie. If I don't book this weekend, I might have real trouble getting you over here. Do you want me to ring his parents? What's his number?"

"No!" Lorna insisted. "I'll sort it out. I'll ring you on Saturday morning, your time."

Joe was due to come over on Friday evening. Mum was going to the theatre with Ric and the couple were having a meal afterwards, so they would be back late. All day at school, Lorna looked forward to the evening. Her mind wasn't on work, but the teachers didn't seem to notice. When they saw that faraway look in her eyes, they assumed that she was concentrating on something relevant.

Sulvinder, however, wasn't so easily fooled.

"Have you done your final Maths assignment yet?" she asked Lorna at lunch.

"Not quite."

Actually, Lorna hadn't even started it. But she found the work easy. She would get it done in an hour over the weekend.

"Mr Bachelor will be dead mad. He won't make an exception because it's you, unlike some other teachers I could mention." The sarcastic tone of Sulvinder's second sentence annoyed Lorna.

"Really!" she snapped at her friend. "You sound worse than Miss Tate. I'll get the work done. It's just that I have other priorities."

"You mean *one* other priority. Joe Green."

"So?"

Sulvinder gave Lorna an awkward but sympathetic look. Then she made a small speech.

"There were reasons, weren't there, why we all said we wouldn't have steady boyfriends until we'd done our exams? Boys can be a real distraction. But you know, if Joe's serious about you, he'll still be waiting when the exams are over."

"What's that supposed to mean?"

Lorna could feel her face going red. She went on.

"Are you trying to imply that Joe and I aren't serious?"

Sulvinder shook her head.

"I'm not trying to imply anything — just to suggest that you might . . . put things into perspective." Her voice became gentle and more tentative.

"I know Joe's your first boyfriend, but he isn't going to be the love of your life, is he? In two years' time, you'll go off to university and leave him behind, if you're still together then."

This was true, Lorna knew. Joe had no interest in higher education. But she wasn't happy about being reminded of this.

"Now you sound like my mother, Sulvinder. How can I think two years in advance? You've got to live for today. I might be knocked over by a bus tomorrow . . ."

"Don't say things like that," Sulvinder said. "I'm not trying to be hurtful. I'm only trying to be your friend. Sometimes friends have to say things that the other one doesn't want to hear."

"Do they?" Lorna asked. "Or is it simply that

you're projecting your own values onto me? Is it that you're worried that Jazz won't wait for you until you're older, but you're too scared of your parents' opinion to go out with him now?"

"That's ridiculous," Sulvinder told her.

"Is it?"

Lorna stared at her friend bitterly. They were on the verge of having a real argument. It would be their first. Lorna thought it better just to walk away.

"I expect you're right," she told Sulvinder. "You know exactly what you're doing with Jazz. I think I'd better go and start that Maths homework, so I've got something to show Mr Bachelor."

She got up and walked away before Sulvinder could reply. When they met up again in the Maths lesson, they would act as though nothing had happened between them. If she was honest with herself, Lorna knew that her friendship with Sulvinder was likely to outlast her relationship with Joe. She would do nothing to risk it. Later, when she'd calmed down, she would apologize for her last outburst.

Yet who could say about her and Joe? Joe could, for instance, get a job in the town where Lorna went to university. They could live together, marry even ... Lorna spent the rest of the lunch hour in a happy daze, thinking about these things. Her Maths book lay forgotten in her bag.

At home that evening, Mum asked when Joe was coming round.

"After you've gone out, I think."

"And he's going to tell you about America tonight?"

"Yes."

Mum gave Lorna the same sympathetic look which Sulvinder had used on her earlier.

"You won't be too disappointed, will you, if he says he can't go? It's a lot of money for a family with three children."

Lorna didn't reply.

"How long have you two been together now? Two months?"

"Ten weeks."

"A lot of first relationships don't last that long. The America holiday's three months away. You may be pushing your luck."

"Dad doesn't think that," Lorna asserted. "Or he wouldn't have invited Joe."

Mum frowned.

"Your father has always been an optimist about matters of the heart. Otherwise he wouldn't have been married three times. Anyway, he doesn't know Joe. He doesn't even know *you* that well."

"Even so, maybe he's right this time."

Lorna had raised her voice. The doorbell rang. It would be Ric, coming to pick Mum up.

"Just try not to be too disappointed if he says no," Mum said, as she put on her coat.

Lorna didn't reply. As her mother went out to meet Ric, she realized that she'd neglected to tell her that she looked good tonight.

Joe was late. The phone rang twice, but each time it was for Ben. *Brookside* was nearly over before the doorbell sounded. Lorna answered it anxiously. Joe stood there, in his bomber jacket, looking sheepish.

"Sorry I'm late. I had to talk to Mum and Dad."

"Of course," Lorna told him. "What did they say?"

She could see the answer on Joe's face before he spoke again.

"I'm sorry," he said. "I tried."

"What did you say?" Lorna asked, shocked. "Did you tell them how much you wanted to go?"

She tried to stop herself crying. Joe began to mumble.

"Money and . . . it's a long time. They say America's really violent and they think I'm too young."

These sounded like really weak reasons to Lorna.

"Can't you make them change their minds?"

"I'm sorry."

Before Lorna could say anything else, Ben came into the room. There was a programme he wanted to watch. Joe and Lorna went up to her room. Joe was withdrawn. When she talked about when they would see each other again over the weekend, he was vague. She guessed that he was as upset about the holiday as she was. He went home early, leaving Lorna to brood over what might have been.

She found it hard to sleep. When Ric and Mum came home she switched her bedside lamp off, so that Mum wouldn't see that she was awake and pop into her room for a chat. But sleep wouldn't come. Lorna thought about Joe and how tongue-tied he'd been tonight. Maybe he'd been the same way in front of his parents. Maybe, if Lorna went round, she could persuade them that it was a good idea. She could make all their fears evaporate. She didn't have to ring her father until six in the evening. She had until then. She rehearsed the conversation with Mr and Mrs Green over and over again in her head, until she was sure that they would have to give in. Then, finally, she fell asleep.

Chapter 16

Lorna avoided her mother in the morning. She didn't want to be asked about whether Joe could go on the holiday. She had breakfast before Mum and Ric were up, then left a note on the kitchen table — "Gone to Joe's". She didn't know Joe's plans for the day and wanted to get to the house before he or his parents went out.

It was a fine morning. Lorna could have caught the bus but decided to walk. As she paced the road from Westtown to Coddington, she went over all the arguments she had come up with to persuade the Greens that they should let Joe go on holiday with her: they wouldn't be travelling anywhere dangerous; her father would find a cheap flight; Joe deserved a good holiday after working hard for his exams.

Somehow, these arguments seemed less convincing in the clear light of morning than they had late last night. But Lorna alternated them with daydreams of the times she and Joe would have in California – scenes in which Ben and her father were conveniently excluded from the picture.

Lorna was in the middle of one of these daydreams when she passed Jazz's house. She nearly didn't notice Abby, who was standing in the doorway with her back to Lorna. Her long hair was swept over her shoulder, and she was wearing her tightest jeans. Lorna wondered what she was doing there. As she blinked in surprise, Jazz opened the door, gave Abby a big smile, and ushered her inside.

This confused Lorna, but she was too preoccupied with Joe and the holiday to think much of it. Soon she was at the Greens' house. Joe's mother answered the door.

"Lorna, you're here bright and early! I don't think Joe's even dressed yet."

"That's OK," Lorna told her. "Actually, it was you and Mr Green I wanted to talk to."

"Really? What about?"

Now that she had to get the words out, Lorna felt awkward. She didn't like delicate situations. She liked to maintain a cool, discreet distance. Embarrassing incidents, like the talk with Miss Tate the other day, made her shudder. But the holiday meant so much to her, and the Greens were a nice couple, who obviously thought that Lorna was a good influence on their son.

"It's about the holidays," Lorna began, as Mrs Green led her into the kitchen.

"Oh yes," said Mrs Green. "Frank? Lorna wants a word with us."

Mr Green put down his *Daily Mail* and smiled at Lorna. In the corner of the room sat Joe's young sister, reading the boys' problem page of *Just Seventeen*. Lorna wished she wasn't there, but there was nothing she could do about it. She began talking.

"It's just that I'd really like Joe to come on holiday with me this summer. I know you've got some misgivings about it but my father would be there all the time and Ben too. Whatever you've heard about America, California's a really safe place and we won't be going to any of the rough areas . . ."

Mr and Mrs Green both looked surprised by this outburst. Even Emily put down her magazine and looked at Lorna oddly. She carried on.

"It won't be that expensive — my father's very good at getting things on the cheap and he'll pay for all the motels and meals and stuff like that. Joe would really enjoy it and . . ."

Her voice trailed off. Mr and Mrs Green were looking at each other with confused expressions. Emily's mouth hung open.

"That's very interesting," Mr Green said, tactfully. "We have talked with Joe about the possibility of his having a holiday on his own, instead of coming with the rest of us to Jersey."

"But would your father and your brother really want Joe around?" Mrs Green asked. "Your father hasn't met him and Joe hasn't got a lot of time for thirteen-year-olds, if his behaviour at home is anything to go by."

"I'm sure they'd get on fine," Lorna answered.

She was surprised by how mild the questioning was. Suddenly, she felt hopeful.

"We'll need to talk about this in private," Mr Green said. "And to talk to Joe and your father, of course."

He smiled.

"But it sounds like a possibility to me."

Lorna grinned from ear to ear. Then she remembered something.

"The only thing is, I need to ring my father at six tonight so that he can book the flights. Evidently they're in very short supply."

The Greens looked at each other.

"That's very short notice," Mrs Green said to Lorna.

"I'm sorry. I did tell Joe ten days ago, but . . ."

Lorna didn't want to criticize Joe, or to remind the Greens that they had already turned down the holiday idea once.

"That's strange," Mr Green said, "because this is the first we've heard about it."

Joe's sister gave a small smile. Lorna felt humiliated as though someone had poured a bucketful of water over her face.

"I think I'd better get Joe," Mrs Green said.

While Lorna waited, Mr Green tried to make conversation with Lorna about her father. What did he do? When had she seen him last? But Lorna couldn't answer coherently. She was too busy trying to work out the extent of Joe's betrayal.

Eventually, her boyfriend came into the kitchen with his mother. He looked angry.

"I think you two need to talk," Mrs Green said. The others left the room.

"What's going on?" Lorna asked, trying to keep her voice down so that nobody could overhear the conversation. "I've just humiliated myself in front of your whole family because of what you told me last night."

"*You've* humiliated yourself?" Joe moaned. "How do you think I feel? You've made me look like a right fool, and a liar."

"I don't understand," Lorna said. "They were perfectly willing to let you go to America with me. Why didn't you ask them?"

Joe didn't reply. There was still sleep in his eyes, Lorna noticed. His hair was all mussed and he wore a T-shirt which had holes in it. He looked very vulnerable. Lorna didn't want to be having this argument. She wanted to cuddle him, to make it right as they had done whenever they had come close to a row before. But this morning, his eyes avoided hers. He looked shifty.

"Surely," she asked gently. "You did *want* to come?"

"No," said Joe, shuffling his feet. "I didn't."

Lorna felt tears welling up in her eyes.

"Why not?" she asked him, trying to hold back the emotion from her voice and failing. "We're in love with each other. You said . . ."

"I meant it," Joe said. The words came out awkwardly, as though he were being strangled. "But . . . but . . . you're not an easy person to go out with. I always feel that I've got to be careful what I say around you, and your friends are worse.

They keep talking over my head and looking at me like I'm an imbecile or something."

"That's ridiculous!" Lorna protested.

Joe looked angry. Now his words came out in a torrent.

"Is it? I'll tell you what's ridiculous. Me, trying to fit in with Abigail Thomas and her fancy friends. Or your mum and her lecturer boyfriend. I feel like I'm having an IQ test every time they try to start a conversation with me. And I'll bet your dad'd be the same. As for you and me, we'd get on each other's nerves within a few days. What's more, there'd be nowhere for me to go off on my own and let off steam. We might be going out with each other at the beginning of the holiday, but I'll bet we wouldn't be by the end of it."

Lorna was crying.

"Why didn't you tell me all this before?"

"Because I didn't want to hurt you."

She looked at him. His voice sounded sincere, but his eyes weren't. Lorna raised her voice.

"You said 'might', we 'might be going out with each other at the beginning of the holiday'. That's what you said, isn't it?"

"I don't remember exactly . . ."

She was almost shouting now.

"Yes, you do. You meant to chuck me before then, didn't you? All these excuses you had ready about me and my family being too clever . . . You'd already made up your mind, hadn't you?"

Joe was silent. Lorna went on. Her voice was taking on a high, accusatory rant. She hated the sound of it, but couldn't stop herself.

"You lied to me. You came to my house last night and told me lies. How could you?"

Joe was embarrassed, Lorna could tell. He wasn't worried about what she was saying. He was worried about the rest of the family overhearing.

"I didn't mean . . ."

Lorna interrupted him.

"Save it for some girl stupid enough to believe all your lies. I've had it with you, Joe Green! You can get lost! If there's one thing I'll regret all my life, it's that you were the first boy I ever . . ."

The words wouldn't come out. Joe came forward. Tenderly, he tried to hold her.

"You were my first too," he said. "Don't end it this way."

Lorna looked at him for a moment. The sincerity in his eyes seemed to mock everything she'd ever felt for him. Lorna was sure, at that moment, that she would never trust another boy again. Tentatively, he touched her hand. Lorna snatched it away. Then she ran out of the house, tears streaming down her face.

"Lorna, what is it?" Mum asked, when she got home.

Lorna didn't speak, but ran upstairs to her room. Later, though, when Mum came in, she told her the story, in between sobs, leaving nothing out.

"You're hurt now," Mum told Lorna, "but you'll be stronger in the long run. It may not seem like much, but that's the only comforting thing I can tell you."

"How could I have fallen in love with him?" Lorna asked. "Why couldn't I realize that he was exactly what I always thought he was – a silly, immature jerk?"

"He seemed like a nice enough boy to me," Mum told Lorna. "Very good looking. Lots of boys fall for girls because of their looks rather than their personality. Why should us women be any different? I think he found himself a bit out of his depth with you, that's all."

She left Lorna alone. Lorna knew that it wasn't her brains which put Joe off, or her family and friends. Joe had dumped her because she wasn't attractive enough and she was too serious all the time – both things that were impossible to change. She hated herself.

What made things worse was that, when she thought about it, she had dumped Joe. Not that she'd had much choice. Joe had put her in a situation where she'd had to chuck him if she was to retain any pride. The scene with his parents had been the most embarrassing of her life.

Downstairs, she heard her mother ringing her father, explaining that it would be just Ben and Lorna coming on holiday in the summer. When she'd finished, Lorna went down and rang Sulvinder. She apologized for the day before, and explained everything that had happened. Sulvinder couldn't come round, because she had a family party to go to, but the two had a long, tearful conversation.

When she'd finished talking to Sulvinder, Lorna rang Abby, but her second-closest friend was out.

Lorna realized that she hadn't mentioned to Sulvinder how she saw Abby at Jazz's. She had forgotten all about it. Still, it was probably best not to worry her friend needlessly. Doubtless there was a perfectly innocent explanation.

Chapter 17

Weeks passed. Lorna tried to throw herself into her work, but found sustained concentration impossible. She hated school and yearned for study leave, which began in the first week of June. English was the worst lesson, because Joe was in the class with her. Their eyes never met. Joe said nothing in these lessons, and neither did Lorna. Miss Tate soon gave up asking her questions.

Media Studies was the only lesson that was tolerable. People sat and talked, did revision, or watched videos. Abby and Sulvinder were sympathetic. They didn't say "I told you so", even though both had been proved right. They encouraged Lorna to get on with her life. Abby gave Lorna what she knew was good advice.

"If you look happy, and do well in your exams, you'll show Joe that you can live without him. He'll see what he's missing."

But this was easier said than done. Other, more

gossipy girls enjoyed seeing Lorna's romance fall flat on its face. Word of the split spread quickly. All the drama queens like Kristi Smythe came running over to offer their sympathies and wheedle the full details out of Lorna. She told them nothing, but this didn't stop rumours spreading, all of them placing Joe, not Lorna, in a favourable light. Lorna hadn't realized how much these girls had envied her.

For a few weeks, she had felt attractive in every way. She had been loved. Now it was over. And, to make things worse, she was forced to see Joe every weekday, even though they never spoke. Lorna felt her femininity fading. She told herself that she was reverting to being the swot she had been before Jazz's party. She was sure that she would never have a boyfriend again.

The only boy who did talk to Lorna was Brian Kane. Brian wasn't interested in her as a girl, only as a fellow enthusiast. They talked about journalism and editing techniques. Brian was one of those boys who lived for nothing but his hobbies. Already, he was working out which courses at university would best equip him for the future. There was a film school in Bristol that he wanted to go to, and then he would take whatever production assistant job he could get hold of, working for nothing if necessary.

"What will you live on?" Lorna asked him.

"I'll sign on, or beg on the streets if I have to," Brian told her. "If you want things in life you've got to be willing to make sacrifices for them."

Lorna was glad to come across someone who

was as obsessed with his career as she was. She would need to be equally obsessive if she was to get into television.

Once, just before study leave, Brian tried to persuade her to go to a film with him. It was about a photographer who kept getting to the scene of the crime before the police. Lorna couldn't decide if Brian had asked her because he was sorry for her, fancied her, or had simply forgotten that she was a girl. She turned him down in the nicest way she could manage. He was an enjoyable person to talk to, but she didn't want people thinking that gangling, long-haired Brian, with his eccentric-looking glasses, was her new boyfriend.

Finally, study leave arrived. Lorna tried to get work done at home, and persuaded her mother that that was what she was doing in her room. But most of the time it wasn't. She played old records, but they no longer meant the same things to her. The songs on *Ingénue*, for instance, which had seemed to be about a fulfilled love, now told of an unrequited one. What had Mum told her? *You'll be stronger next time.* It was true. But Lorna didn't want to be strong, if it meant being hard. She wanted that delicious melting feeling again. She wanted to feel that unexpected passion, that feeling of amazing luck and lightness. She wanted Joe.

But Joe didn't want her. Two days before the exams began, Lorna went to the library to find some books about Sylvia Plath. The American poet was the one they'd studied in English and Lorna didn't have full notes on all the poems. She'd expected to work them out for herself later, but there were two or three she couldn't understand.

It was early evening. Lorna was just leaving the library. There was a warm, fresh breeze, announcing the imminent arrival of summer, which pleased her. Then she saw two familiar people getting off the bus from Coddington, hand in hand.

It was Joe and a girl Lorna vaguely recognized from the fourth year. Her name was Tracey or Stacey. She wore black stockings and a short skirt, revealing legs that went all the way up to her tight waist, which Joe now had his arm around. Lorna felt physically sick. She grabbed onto the rail by the library steps.

"Are you all right, dear? You're trembling."

An old man stood by, looking at her with concern.

"I . . . had a shock. I'll be fine."

The old man insisted on helping her down the steps. When Lorna looked up, Joe and his bimbo companion were nearly out of sight, turning into the entrance of the cinema where Joe and Lorna had had their first date.

"Are you sure you'll be all right?"

The old man brought his wrinkled, kindly face close to hers, as if trying to see where the damage lay. Lorna shook her head.

"No. I'll never be all right again."

As the man looked at her in sympathetic confusion, Lorna dropped her books and ran all the way home.

After that evening, Lorna found revision almost

impossible. The exams began and she took them in a kind of daze. She answered all the questions, but when Abby and Sulvinder were discussing the papers afterwards, she found that she couldn't remember the points they were analysing so keenly. In her best subject, English Literature, she was able to concentrate better. But then she had a disaster as she tried to answer the last question, on Shakespeare's *A Midsummer-Night's Dream*.

The question she chose to answer was, *"The path of true love never did run smooth* – How far would you say that the play justifies this statement?"* Lorna knew how to answer the question – she knew the play backwards – and was only a little behind on time. All she had to do was jot down her rough plan, then she would have no trouble in completing the essay in the half-hour she had remaining. But she couldn't get it together. She knew how to structure the essay: she simply had to show how the whole play revolved around love complications, adding, for extra depth, that there was more to it than that. But she couldn't take it seriously.

It all seemed so stupid: a king who won his wife in battle; lovers so unsure of their feelings that they required love potions to help them see the light; and a plot that only worked because of the intervention of fairies. The only good thing about the play, the way she felt today, was the "rude mechanicals" – the workmen who were putting on a play within a play, parodying the whole thing. Shakespeare, she thought, knew that he was writing a bit of dross – a crowd-pleaser – and used these workmen to show that he knew.

Lorna started trying to write this argument, but the words kept failing her. Every time she came to the word "love", her mind turned to Joe. He was sitting two chairs ahead of her and had stopped writing. English wasn't one of his best subjects. He had probably run out of things to say. She could see the nape of his neck, which she had stroked and kissed so many times. How could she write about love in the abstract when the boy she loved was sitting only five feet from her and he was going out with someone else?

"Lorna? Are you all right?"

Miss Tate, who was invigilating the exam, leant over Lorna and whispered urgently. Lorna blinked and stared at her blankly.

"What?"

Miss Tate's voice was kind.

"You're crying, Lorna. Look, there are tear stains all over your essay."

Lorna looked down. It was true. The paragraph she had written about the play was illegible. Tears had blurred her words, making them bleed down the page. Miss Tate gave her a tissue.

"Is something wrong? Would you like me to take you to the toilet so that you can wash your face?"

Without replying, Lorna stood up. There was no point in continuing with the exam. She could not finish the question she had started and had no time to begin another one. She dropped her tissue next to her exam paper, then, leaving her pen behind, walked out of the exam hall.

Miss Tate followed her. Lorna didn't want to talk to the teacher and kept on walking. Then, as she came to the foyer doors she realized that she hadn't picked up her bag. It would be humiliating to come back for it later, when everyone else was finishing the exam. She turned round, expecting to have to face Miss Tate. But the teacher was dealing with someone else.

It was Joe. Miss Tate was speaking to him, in a low but commanding voice.

"You can't just walk out of an exam."

"Why not?" Joe asked indignantly. "She did. And I want to talk to her."

Lorna went to the pile of bags and pulled hers out from under it.

Miss Tate continued. "Lorna's not well, and I suspect that you have something to do with what's depressing her. Get back into the hall now!"

"No," Joe told her. "I've finished the exam. You can't make me stay."

"Oh, yes I can," Miss Tate insisted. "The exam regulations say . . ."

Lorna didn't wait to find out what the exam regulations said, or to see if Joe managed to get past the English teacher. She walked out of the building and breathed in the fresh June air. It was all over. This had been her last exam.

She didn't know whether she'd done badly or well in the other exams, and she no longer cared. All she knew was that her young heart had broken as easily as a china cup, and the pieces were so small and splintered that no glue would ever put it back together again. All she wanted now was to get away.

Interlude

The flight to San Francisco took eight hours. Ben managed to doze off for much of it, but Lorna found herself restlessly awake. She tried to watch the films being shown in the centre of the aisle, but both were terrible. For the first four hours, she ranged through the magazines on the rack. Then she tried the book which Mum had urged on her – a novel by Armistead Maupin set in the city she was about to visit. The book was a good choice. It was light and funny and made her want to see San Francisco. It was the first time she'd felt that way since she'd split up with Joe.

When she closed *Tales of the City*, there was less than an hour to go. Ben woke up and immediately became excited.

"How far's the airport from the city? What kind of car's Dad got? How much time do you think he'll spend with us?"

Lorna didn't know the answer to any of these questions. She began to think about how she would get on with her father. It had been a long time since she'd spent more than a weekend with him.

But Ben didn't give Lorna much time to think. He kept chattering, making her realize how tired she was. It was nearly midnight, according to her body clock. But Ben was wide awake.

"Do you think we'll go over the Golden Gate Bridge today? Will you help me to persuade Dad to take us to Yosemite Park? A friend of mine's been there. They have bears, just wandering around. Can you believe that?"

Lorna assured him that she wanted to go there

too and, to her relief, her brother went quiet. Ben seemed less secure about the holiday than she was. He sounded like a ten-year-old, not a boy who had just turned fourteen.

"Lorna," he said after a while.

"What?"

Lorna hoped this wasn't going to be another silly question.

"I'm glad that it's just you. I mean, I'm sorry about you and Joe, but I'm glad he isn't coming on holiday with us."

Lorna wasn't sure what to think of this.

"Why?"

Ben smiled sheepishly.

"Because you'll have to talk to me. If Joe was coming, I'd be on my own all the time, or with Dad."

"Maybe you'd enjoy spending a lot of time with Dad."

"Maybe."

He didn't sound convinced. Ben had spent less time with their father than she had. Lorna could dimly remember her mother and father living together. Ben couldn't. She had been so preoccupied with her own problems that she hadn't thought about Ben's. Boys were expected to get on better with their fathers than their mothers. It was an additional pressure on Ben.

"Don't worry," she told her brother. "I'll talk to you."

"I reckon Dad'll be away on business a lot — that's what Mum says. You won't spend all your time reading, will you? We can go places together."

"Yes," said Lorna, smiling at him. "We can go places."

Once they had picked up their luggage from the baggage carousel, Lorna and Ben still had to queue for a long time before they got through immigration. Then, at last, they were out. Lorna suddenly felt lost. People were milling around her. Suppose her father wasn't there to meet them?

"There he is!"

Dad was wearing a short-sleeved shirt and tinted glasses. He was walking towards them with a big smile on his face. Ben ran up to him. They hugged. Then he and Lorna were face to face.

"It's been a long time, sweetheart."

He kissed her. She could smell his aftershave. Awkwardly, she pressed her body against his in a hug.

"My, you've grown!"

He took over the baggage trolley and wheeled it towards the car-parking area. Ben walked alongside him, talking fast. Dad answered all of his questions in the affirmative. Lorna struggled to keep up with them. She felt as if she was walking in her sleep.

The jet lag took Lorna longer to get over than it did Ben. She had a short sleep as soon as she got to the hotel, then couldn't get to sleep for ages that night. At least she had a room to herself, and could read without disturbing anybody. Now and then she looked out of her window at the people still walking by in Washington Square.

The next day, Dad took them to Union Square in the centre of the city, and Chinatown. They rode a trolley car up and down steep hills and gazed over towards the bay and the Golden Gate Bridge. In the evening they wandered around the area where they were staying – North Beach. Lorna was amazed to find a huge bookshop, City Lights, which was open until midnight. She bought a new Sylvia Plath biography, along with the rest of the *Tales of the City* books to read on her holiday. Ben was more impressed to find a whole restaurant devoted to courses flavoured with garlic.

Dad insisted on buying Lorna a pair of Ray-Ban sunglasses, which were a fraction of the price she'd pay in Britain. She loved the way she looked in them, but there was a problem.

"They're great, Dad. But I can hardly see with them on."

"I could get you prescription ones, I suppose," Dad mused. "No, I've got a better idea. Those round glasses of yours make you look like some kind of pseudo-intellectual. Let's get you fitted with contact lenses."

Lorna put up a little argument, but Dad told her she was being silly. In Britain, she would have had to arrange separate appointments for a fitting and an eye test. Here, it was all done in half an hour. The optician apologized that Lorna would have to wait until Monday. Normally they had same-day service, but since it was late on

Saturday afternoon, she would have to wait.

On Sunday, Dad took them to Golden Gate Park, a sprawling, windy space, full of people, too vast to explore fully. They went to the museum and the Japanese Tea Gardens, then ate their picnic lunch listening to a free concert by a samba group. Lorna found herself beginning to relax for the first time in months. San Francisco seemed so much more free and easy than Westtown. And Joe was thousands of miles away. She no longer had to worry about how to act whenever she bumped into him.

Later that afternoon the three of them took a long walk along Haight Street, which was full of record shops and book shops and people who seemed to think that the nineteen-sixties were still going on.

"What do you think of it so far?" Dad asked.

"It's terrific," Lorna told him. "We could stay here for the whole four weeks. There's so much to see."

"Unfortunately," Dad told her, "I have to be in Sonoma tomorrow. But we'll come back for a couple of days at the end of the holiday, I promise."

On Monday morning, after picking up Lorna's lenses, they drove over the Golden Gate Bridge to Sonoma. At first Lorna had avoided any detailed conversations with her father. Once they were in the car, that became impossible. However, Ben was there too, stopping Dad asking questions that were very personal. But Ben had a habit of falling asleep in the car.

"Got a new boyfriend yet?" he asked Lorna.

"Too busy with my exams," Lorna muttered, embarrassed.

"You're so pretty these days, I know it won't be long."

Lorna shrugged. The contact lenses made her eyes sting. She didn't feel any prettier.

Yet, as she explored the old town's large square, she noted one or two men giving her a second glance and smiled to herself. Maybe the girl who had finished with Joe still had some sex appeal. Or maybe it was just her new sunglasses.

That night they stopped in a rich spa town called Calistoga. The cosy house they stayed in described itself as a bed and breakfast, but Dad moaned that it cost more than the hotel in San Francisco. The next morning they went to look at a natural geyser, called Old Faithful, because it erupted every forty minutes precisely. The water shot over thirty metres in the air. While Lorna took photographs, Ben rushed forward and put his hand into the pool of water.

"Watch out for rocks!" Dad called.

Ben lifted up his hand.

"It's hot!" he shouted. "Come and feel."

As the geyser's stream spluttered down to a trickle, Lorna went and put her hand in the water. Ben splashed her and she splashed him back.

"Hey, you two! Stop that!"

Lorna laughed, then stopped. She was wondering if Joe would have done the same thing as her brother. Then she realized something. This was the first time she had thought about Joe that morning. She hadn't dreamt about him last night, either. A whole twelve hours had gone by without her thinking about Joe Green once. Maybe she really was on the way to getting over him.

They travelled east, nearly as far as Nevada. The climate became hotter and dustier, making Lorna's lenses even less comfortable, but she stuck with them. Dad had to work most days. However, he left them plenty of money. Sometimes Lorna would go shopping, look at the sights with Ben. Other times, she would sit around the motel, reading, or, if there was a pool, go for a swim.

Her costume was a tight one-piece which was a year old. Lorna had filled out a lot since she got it. Dad kept telling her to buy a new one, and she soon did. The looks she got from young men annoyed and embarrassed her. A couple of them tried to chat her up. They told her that her English accent was "cute", but Lorna didn't think it was her accent they were talking about.

The following week she had her one real brush with romance on the holiday. As Dad had promised, they stayed in a cabin in Yosemite Park, a vast forest the size of an English county, with a spectacular mountain range in the centre. The mountain air suited Lorna. Her eyes had finally adapted to the contact lenses and she had developed a healthy tan from lounging around beside swimming pools. She felt a different person.

At Yosemite, Dad struck up a friendship with

a mid-western American, who was, like him, a divorcee taking his kids on holiday. This man had two boys — Michael and Drew — who were the same age as Lorna and Ben. The four of them rented bicycles and explored the park while the two men went walking on their own.

Michael was a tall, fair-haired boy, good looking in a gaunt sort of way. He reminded Lorna of someone, but she couldn't think who. After they'd been cycling for an hour, Drew suggested that they separate. The reason he gave was incredibly unconvincing. Lorna could see what was going on, but let Ben and Drew go off, anyway. She found Michael kind of attractive, and had nothing to lose.

Lorna and Michael cycled to Mirror Lake, a thin, narrow pool at the side of a small mountain. At its head was a five-metre rock, shaped like a knight from a chess set, which appeared to be guarding the pool. Lorna stared at the reflection of the mountains in the still, clear waters. This was clearly a popular spot with tourists, but it was late in the afternoon and most of them were gone.

"Tired?" Michael asked.

"A little."

"Why don't we rest here? It's a good place to sit."

They found some long grass and lay down. Michael wasn't terribly good with conversation. Lorna found it easier to talk to him than he did to her. She liked that.

"Do you have a boyfriend back in England?" Michael asked, as she knew he would.

"No. How about you?"

"No one special."

"That's good," Lorna said. "We needn't feel guilty then."

She let him kiss her. His kisses were different from Joe's, more urgent, but that was kind of nice.

When he showed signs of getting too involved, Lorna told him to back off.

"What's wrong?" Michael asked.

"I'm not ready for a strong romance."

"Why?" he asked gently, stroking her blouse.

"I don't have a boyfriend, but I'm just getting over someone. I'm not ready for more than this."

"That's OK."

She kissed him again. Just saying those words − *I'm getting over someone* − seemed to make them come true. Lorna *was* getting over Joe. Two days later, she was sorry to say goodbye to Michael when their four days in the park were over. But not that sorry. Michael insisted that he'd write, but Lorna knew he wouldn't. And, if he did, she wasn't sure she'd reply.

The only depressing part of the holiday was on August the sixteenth, when Lorna rang home for her exam results. Instead of the several top grades she'd been expected to get, she only had one, for Media Studies. She'd done all the coursework for that before she'd even started going out with Joe. She'd managed a B in English and a C in English Literature (despite not finishing the exam), with more Cs in the rest. Most people would have been satisfied with that, but, for a day, Lorna felt like a failure.

However, she was on holiday, and it was impossible to be depressed for long. After the four days in Yosemite, the holiday seemed to be over far too quickly. They stayed in Hollywood and Santa Barbara and travelled up the Pacific Coast highway, visiting Big Sur and Monterey. Before they knew it, the three of them were back in San Francisco again, buying presents for the people at home.

Although they had spent nearly four weeks together, Lorna didn't really feel that she had got to know her father well. Maybe Ben had. The two usually shared a room and Lorna could sense a growing closeness between them in the way that they joked and argued. But Lorna kept her distance.

Dad was constantly joking, and referring to his vast retinue of girlfriends, but he rarely talked about his feelings or the past. Lorna liked him, but could not imagine what it would be like to live with him all the time. He reminded her of Ric. There was something slightly shallow about him. Maybe her mother kept going for the same kind of man: one who had a personality which was attractive but evasive. Only when they were saying their goodbyes and talking about how much they'd miss each other did Lorna realize who her father resembled even more closely: Joe.

Flying back to England, the time difference was even more severe – sixteen hours. They left San Francisco in the afternoon, and when they returned, it was early morning. Mum met them at the airport. She wanted to know everything about their holiday, but Lorna was too tired to tell her. By the time they got into Mum's car, her body clock registered two in the morning. As Ben wittered on about all the places they'd visited, Lorna spread herself out over the back seat and fell asleep.

Part 2

Chapter 18

The Sixth Form college was an old, red-brick building in the centre of Westtown. It drew students from the town and all the surrounding villages, including Coddington. On registration day, Lorna recognized quite a few people from her old school, but the majority of faces were new, which was good. She wanted to be able to make a fresh start, to be a new person. Today she looked different and felt different too.

"Lorna! Hi! I didn't recognize you at first."

Lorna smiled at the tall boy behind her in the Communication Studies queue.

"I didn't recognize you, either."

It was Brian Kane, from her old school. His hair was cut shorter and he was wearing new glasses.

"You look great," he told her. "Where did you get that tan?"

"California. How did you do in your GCSEs?"

Brian, predictably, had got better grades than she had. All of Lorna's friends had got better grades than her (unless she counted Joe, who was no longer a friend).

"What other subjects are you doing?" she asked Brian.

"Art and History. How about you?"

"Art and English Lit. So I expect we'll end up in the same group for one or the other."

She stepped forward to sign up, which only took a moment.

"See you around!"

Lorna went to find Sulvinder, who was in the Physics line.

"Have you seen Abby?"

Sulvinder shook her head. Neither of them had seen much of Abby recently.

"But I *have* seen someone else," Sulvinder added. She pointed to the front of the queue, where the back of Joe Green's head was bending down over a registration form. Then he stood. Joe was wearing a familiar cream jacket. Lorna gazed at his profile as he walked towards the Biology line. All he had to do was incline his head just slightly in her direction, and he would see her. Lorna felt goose pimples all down her spine. All of the things she had convinced herself of on holiday no longer seemed true. She'd been kidding herself. She wasn't over him. She was still . . .

Then he was out of the danger area, lost in the sea of people. Lorna breathed a sigh of relief. It was just a momentary panic attack, she told herself. She was over him, really. Only she wasn't ready to face him just yet, that was all.

Finally, Lorna found Abby in the English Literature line.

"Hello, stranger!"

The two had seen each other only once since Lorna's return. For as long as Lorna could remember, they had had these gaps in their friendship. Abby was always developing new, intense relationships which lasted a few months then burnt out. The most recent one had been with Melissa. Melissa, however, had decided to stay on at Westtown Comp. From what Lorna could gather, Abby had dropped Mel ruthlessly after the exams. Lorna wondered who Abby had found to hang out with now.

There was one possibility, but that was too radical for Lorna to contemplate: Abby could have found herself a boyfriend.

"Your suntan hasn't started to fade yet," Abby commented.

Lorna was keeping it up with her mother's sun lamp, but didn't tell Abby this. Abby held the opinion that if it wasn't natural, it wasn't worth it. But Lorna wasn't as afraid of Abby's opinion as she had once been. She pointed to a poster.

"Are you going to come to the New Faces disco tonight?"

Abby shrugged disdainfully.

"I don't know. Are you?"

"Why not? We're new faces, aren't we?"

"I suppose so."

Abby didn't like being in any situation she wasn't in control of.

"So, you'll come?"

"OK. I'll meet you here."

Abby turned to join the Politics line. She planned to read Politics, Philosophy and Economics at Oxford, and was studying Politics and Economics at college because she thought that doing the subjects at A level would give her a head start. As she walked off, she called over her shoulder to Lorna.

"Your friend Joe'll be there. Have you decided what you'll do if he asks you for a second go?"

Lorna blushed, but didn't answer. She found herself thinking about Abby's question as she queued to register for Art, the longest line yet. Of course, Lorna had had fantasies about Joe seeing her the way she looked now and begging her to go out with him again. But they were only fantasies. Real life never conformed to your daydreams. And, if Joe had been telling the truth, their break-up had nothing to do with a lack of physical attraction. It was more a matter of intellect and personality.

Lorna felt that she *had* changed while she was over in America. She had learnt to "lighten up", as they said in California. Maybe she would keep changing. Now that she was at college, there was no need for her to fit the "brainy, boring" stereotype everyone had plugged her into at Westtown Comp. But her poor exam results embarrassed her. She meant to make sure that she got excellent A levels, proving that her mediocre GCSEs were a mere hiccup. Whoever her next boyfriend was, he would have to understand that schoolwork came first. Lorna couldn't see Joe accepting that.

And yet. And yet. Just the sight of his back a

few minutes ago had started her heart churning, and it still hadn't stopped. She couldn't help thinking that the two of them had unfinished business.

"Your name, please?"

Lorna blinked and looked at the woman behind the desk. Somehow, she had managed to arrive at the front of the queue.

"Lorna. Lorna Haines. H-A-I-N-E-S."

Chapter 19

Lorna had only been to youth club discos before. After a couple of these, she and Sulvinder had agreed that they were not their scene. Abby had no interest in going along to those meat markets either. But that was then and this was now. Lorna wanted to meet some new people. Sulvinder had agreed to come. What most surprised Lorna was that Abby had, too.

As soon as Lorna and Sulvinder arrived in the students' union hall, they spotted Abby, on the edge of the dance floor, surrounded by boys, as usual. She wore a simple, long black sweater, which, with a black leather belt round the middle, doubled as a dress. She wore black tights too. The overall effect of all this was to draw even more attention to her long, luxuriant brown hair.

But Lorna no longer felt shown up by her friend's good looks. She and Sulvinder both wore jeans and a "body". Now that Lorna had some kind of figure she wanted to show it to full advantage. Seeing them, Abby waved. Then she walked away from her retinue of admirers and joined her friends.

"Is Jazz coming tonight?" she asked.

Sulvinder shook her head.

"He'd feel out of place, he said."

"Weren't you tempted to stay at the Comp, too?" Abby enquired.

"Not really. They're good on languages, which is why he stayed, but I couldn't bear to have the same science teachers for another two years."

Sulvinder knew that Abby knew this already, but she wasn't going to give anything away about her relationship with Jazz. Even Lorna wasn't quite sure how it stood. Sulvinder seemed determined that it should stay secret from her parents, but it wasn't a secret from Jazz's mum and dad, as Sulvinder went round there often. Sometimes Lorna had to cover for her. As Abby talked to Sulvinder, Lorna remembered having seen Abby arrive at Jazz's house months before. Whatever the reason for the visit, Abby had never mentioned it.

The three girls sipped pineapple juice and lemonade, talking about who had come to the college and who had stayed at the comp. All the while they were watching the dance floor from the edge of the bar. Tonight, Lorna felt like dancing. She spent too much of her time observing, analysing what was going on. That way, you missed the fun. It was easy to be cynical, as Abby was now, describing the predatory older students — some of whom must be retaking courses for the second time – getting ready to pounce on innocent sixteen-year-olds. Observers might feel superior, but they missed all the fun.

"Let's dance," Lorna suggested, putting down her glass.

"Sure," Sulvinder said.

Abby looked more hesitant, but muttered "OK," and followed them down the stairs from the bar.

Some girls stood on the edge of the dance floor, as Abby had earlier, talking with friends or being chatted up. Boys went up to them and tried their luck. Other people, of both sexes, got onto the floor and danced. This was what the three girls did now, not caring that they didn't have male partners. It was dancing for the sake of dancing.

Soon, boys began to come up to the three girls and dance close by them. In this situation, Lorna worked out, you had several choices. You could turn away, dancing in an ever tighter knot with your friends and cutting the boy off. Or you could pretend he wasn't there, forcing him to move closer, move away, or try a chat-up line (not easy, as the music was loud). Finally, if you liked, you could smile at the boy and dance with him, checking him out all the time. Sooner or later, he would offer to buy you a drink and you got to find out if he could talk as well as dance.

"What did we used to call these things at the old youth club?" Abby asked. "*Meat Markets?*"

"Don't worry," Lorna teased her. "Everybody can see your 'Not For Sale' sign."

The funny thing was that, as they were dancing, it wasn't Abby who the boys kept dancing closer to, but Lorna. Maybe, she thought, I look more approachable. None of the boys particularly caught her eye, so she kept a certain distance from them. But she was flattered all the same. Then a familiar voice spoke.

"I know I look embarrassing when I do this, but you three are the first friendly faces I've seen since I've got here."

The voice belonged to Brian Kane. It was true, he couldn't dance well. He was too tall and gangly and had no sense of rhythm. Instead of attaching himself to Lorna or Sulvinder, he danced in the middle of the three girls, self-consciously smiling. Lorna took pity on him.

"Come on, Brian, my feet are tired. Let me buy you a drink."

They left the other two girls dancing. Brian insisted on getting the drinks, and when Lorna accused him of being a chauvinist, he pointed out that he was a foot taller than her and would get served much more easily. Then they sat in one of the quieter corners of the bar and talked.

Brian, it turned out, had been to America on holiday too, visiting relations in the midwest.

"It feels kind of weird, doesn't it?" Brian said. "Coming back to this dump."

"Oh, I think the college is OK," Lorna told him. "Better than the comp, anyway."

"I don't mean that the college is a dump," Brian said. "I mean Westtown. It's so dreary and provincial. I mean this whole country. It's grey and boring and everyone's so small-minded and afraid of any kind of success. Do you know what I mean?"

"I suppose so," Lorna replied. "You sound more cynical than Abby."

Brian shook his head.

"Nah. Abby's an English stereotype. She sneers at everything because she's afraid of people sneering at her. She's typical lower middle class, clinging on to a tiny bit of status."

"That's my friend you're talking about," Lorna protested.

Brian swiftly backtracked.

"Don't get me wrong. I like her. But it's a pity she's got the looks of one of those plastic models in American daytime soap operas. I mean, what boy is going to go near her for her brains?"

Lorna laughed. She hadn't really thought about Abby in those terms before. Brian had almost succeeded in making Lorna feel sorry for her.

Brian went to get more drinks. Lorna insisted that he use her money. She wondered what had happened to Abby and Sulvinder, but wasn't worried. She was enjoying talking as much as she had enjoyed dancing. It wasn't as though she was on the lookout for a boyfriend – not yet. She was more concerned about making a good start to her A levels.

Someone tapped her on the shoulder. Lorna turned round with a smile, thinking that it was Brian, passing her her drink.

"Long time no see."

It was Joe, grinning his familiar grin, looking handsome in a new shirt.

"Are you with someone?"

"Sort of," Lorna muttered.

As soon as these words were out, Lorna regretted them. She should have said yes or no, not been evasive. But seeing Joe again was a shock. Part of her wanted to tell him where to go. The other part wanted to embrace him. It wanted to press her body against his and have him whispering sweet, meaningless words in her ear. Instead, she asked, in a cold voice.

"Where's Tracey?"

Joe looked surprised.

"You mean Stacey?" He stumbled over the words. "I didn't know you knew about her. She's history. You know, you look terrific. What happened to your glasses?"

"Lenses."

"America must have been good for you. Hey, listen . . ."

He had sat down now, without being asked, and was leaning close to her.

"I'm really sorry about the way we split up. I should never have lied to you like I did. I handled the whole thing really badly."

"Yes," said Lorna, "you did."

"I'm not like that really. You know that."

His eyes were sincere. Lorna would have liked to melt straight into his arms. But she had her pride.

"If you say so," she mumbled, grudgingly.

"So, can we be friends?"

He offered her his hand, in a mock English gentleman way.

"OK," Lorna told him. "Friends."

Joe began burbling away about the courses he

was doing, the mess he'd made of his exams and the boring time he'd had with his family on Jersey. Then he gave an irritated look over Lorna's shoulder. Lorna turned round. She'd forgotten all about Brian.

"Here's your drink," the tall boy said. "And your change."

Lorna thanked him, and tried to think of what to say next. But before she could say another word, Brian walked back into the crowd he had emerged from. Lorna started to get up to go after him, but Joe put his hand over hers.

"I see what you meant," he said in his casual, mocking way. "*Sort of.*"

Chapter 20

Joe looked into her eyes. All of the old flame was there. If anything, he was better looking now than he had been in the spring. He was just that little bit older, and had a new haircut. It would be very easy, Lorna knew, to fall for him again if he kept encouraging her. It would be very easy for him to break her heart a second time: the heart she had only just finished putting back together. She had to be strong. He would never respect her if she just melted into his arms as though nothing had gone wrong between them. Yet she wanted him so much.

"Do you want to dance?" he asked, as he had asked back in March.

"Another time." Lorna stood up. "I'm here to meet some new people. That's what this disco's all about, isn't it?"

Joe looked rebuffed, but quickly recovered his composure.

"You're right," he said. "I'll see you around."

The minute he was gone, Lorna regretted

turning him down. But she had her pride. If he wanted her back, he would have to prove himself. She walked back towards the dance floor.

"There you are!"

It was Sulvinder and Abby.

"Where's Brian?" Abby asked. "I didn't realize he was your type."

Lorna smiled.

"We had a good time exchanging holiday anecdotes until Joe came along."

She told them about her conversation with Joe, all the time looking around to see if she could spot Brian. He was a friend and she didn't want to offend him. But Brian was nowhere to be seen. A boy who Sulvinder knew came over and insisted on buying her and Abby drinks. Then a tall, dark-haired boy came over and asked Lorna to dance.

"Why not?" she said.

The three girls spent the rest of the evening dancing.

"And was *he* there?" Mum asked, when Lorna got home.

She nodded.

"And?"

"We talked. He asked me to dance."

"And?"

"I said 'no' politely."

Mum grinned.

"Good for you!"

"Anyway," Lorna said, "there were plenty of other boys who wanted to dance with me."

"Seeing any of them again?"

Lorna shrugged.

"We'll see."

"Once bitten, twice shy?" Mum suggested.

Lorna thought about it.

"I don't think so," she said. "Just cautious. What's the hurry?"

Term started the following day. It was very strange, being in new classes and hardly knowing anybody there. Brian Kane was in Lorna's Communication Studies group. She sat next to him and they talked amicably about movies and courses. He didn't seem to have taken offence from the previous night's interrupted conversation.

At home, Lorna found time to start reading novels again, as avidly as she had before starting to go out with Joe. The latest was one that Ric had recommended to her: *Lady Audley's Secret* by Mary Elizabeth Braddon. Reading these century-old romances took Lorna out of herself. She didn't mind the implausible coincidences and bizarre moral codes which Ric sometimes criticized. She never tired of the mad women locked away in the attic. Lorna thought of herself as a bit of a mad woman. Sometimes it seemed as though so little had changed. If you were intelligent and you were a girl, it was best not to show it, or you would scare your lovers away, as she had Joe.

When she'd finished the first volume of the book, she felt like chatting with someone. She rang Sulvinder. Her friend wasn't there.

"Lorna?" Her mother sounded confused. "Isn't

she round at your house? That's where she said she was going."

Lorna cursed herself. She'd forgotten that Sulvinder was seeing Jazz tonight and had told her parents that she was with her. She had to improvise.

"Yes," she said. "That's why I'm calling, to see if she was still coming round. I think she must have bumped into somebody . . ."

"Now you've got me worried. She's been gone nearly an hour. Suppose . . ."

"I'm sure it's nothing," Lorna said. "I'll tell you what – I'll get her to give you a call as soon as she arrives. OK?"

"Yes. Please do that."

Lorna put down the phone, then immediately looked up Jazz's number. She hoped that he and Sulvinder were spending the evening at his house, otherwise there could be some embarrassing consequences. But before she could dial Jazz, the phone rang. Lorna answered it, hoping that the caller might be Sulvinder. It wasn't. It was Brian Kane.

"I was wondering . . ."

Brian sounded nervous. Lorna didn't have time for him to spend ages getting round to whatever he wanted to get round to.

"I'm sorry, Brian. There's this important call I was just about to make. Can I call you back or is it . . ."

Brian spoke quickly.

"It's just that I was reading the evening paper and I saw that the new Almodovar film we were talking about opens at the Showcase tomorrow. I wondered if you'd like to go tomorrow night."

"Oh, OK. Maybe. I don't see why . . . Can I tell you at college tomorrow?"

"Sure. I just thought you'd like some notice."

"Yes. Fine. I'll see you tomorrow."

She put the phone down, then hesitated before she called Jazz. Now that she'd said "maybe", it would be much harder to turn Brian down, the way she had last time he'd asked her out. But why should she turn him down? He was a nice bloke and he was interesting company. They liked the same kind of films. All right, she didn't fancy him as much as she did Joe, but sex appeal wasn't everything. And the new-look Brian was quite good looking, in a gawky sort of way. He reminded her of someone, though she couldn't think who. And it was only a date. Maybe he didn't even think of it as a date, more just going to a movie with a friend.

But Brian could wait. Lorna dialled Jazz's number. The phone was engaged. She left it two minutes, then phoned again. Still engaged. Some people, Lorna knew, could talk on the phone for hours. Probably it was Jazz's younger sister, Pamelajit. Or maybe it was his dad, sorting out a film deal. From what Jazz had told her, Bill Jones often worked around the clock, not sleeping if there wasn't time. She tried the number once more. Still engaged.

Before long, Sulvinder's mother would ring again, Lorna was sure. What should she say? There was no easy answer. She could walk over to Jazz's house, but the fastest she could do it in would be half an hour. Surely, whoever it was would be off the phone within that time? Alternatively, she could take a taxi. She probably had enough money. But suppose Jazz and Sulvinder weren't there? Or suppose Sulvinder's mum rang while Lorna was out? Lorna couldn't see Ben telling very convincing lies to her. Nor would she want to ask him to.

Lorna dialled the number again. Still engaged. Almost the moment she put the phone down, it began to ring. She jumped. Should she pick it up? Suppose it was Sulvinder's mum? She didn't want to talk to her. But on the other hand, if Mrs Kaur got no answer, she would probably think the worst anyway. Reluctantly, Lorna picked up the phone.

It was Joe.

"I'm sorry we're not in any of the same classes," he told her. "I was looking forward to getting another chance to talk to you today."

"Maybe we'll meet up in General Studies tomorrow," she told him.

Actually, she knew they would. She'd looked at the group lists on the notice board earlier.

"Oh, General Studies is optional," Joe said. "I'm not sure I'll bother going to the classes."

Typical Joe!

"I was thinking . . ." he went on.

"Unusual for you," Lorna quipped.

"Yeah. Right. I was thinking, if you weren't doing anything on Saturday night, maybe we could . . ."

"Are you asking me for a date, Joe Green?"

Joe sounded embarrassed.

"Call it a quasi-date if you like; you know — an attempt at reconciliation."

"That's a six-syllable word, Joe. You'd better watch it. People will accuse you of being an intellectual."

"Ah, come on, Lorna. I still feel really bad about the way we ended. Don't make me beg, huh?"

Lorna found that she rather enjoyed the prospect of making him beg. But she had another, more urgent decision to make.

"Look, Joe, I'll have to think about it. But could you do me a big favour. . . ?"

Joe lived less than five minutes' walk from Jazz's house. Lorna explained the situation, asking Joe to go round and alert Sulvinder to her predicament.

"And if I do this," Joe asked, "will you go out with me on Saturday?"

"I told you," Lorna said. "I'll think about it. Now will you please go round to Jazz's?"

"I'm on my way."

Ten minutes later the phone rang again. It was Sulvinder.

"Thanks, Lorna. You saved my life."

"Don't thank me. I caused the problem in the first place. Thank Joe."

"I already did. Jazz is giving him a beer."

"What did you tell your mother?"

"I said the first thing that came into my mind — that when I was walking over to your house, I bumped into your ex-boyfriend, Joe, and he took me for a coffee, then kept asking me how to get you to go out with him again."

"And she believed that?"

"Sure. She wasn't very happy about me being in a café on my own with a white boy. 'Think about your reputation', she said. But that's OK. The fact that I knew she wouldn't approve makes it a more convincing excuse."

"What are you going to do now?"

"Are you on your own?"

"Yes. Mum's out for the evening."

"Why don't I get Jazz to drive me over? Mum said that she'd get Dad to pick me up on the way back from the temple, which won't be until ten."

"OK," Lorna said. "Fine."

Five minutes later, Sulvinder was there. She got out of the car with Jazz beside her.

"I thought I'd bring Jazz in for a few minutes," she said. "He was complaining that he hardly ever sees you."

"Great," Lorna said.

"Oh, and I've brought somebody else as well."

A grinning figure got out of the back seat. It was Joe.

Chapter 21

Joe sat in the corner of Lorna's bedroom, silent. Jazz talked about the university place that he wanted to take up the next year.

"Oxford?" Lorna said. "Abby wants to go there."

Jazz gave Lorna a slightly strange look.

"Which college?" Lorna asked. "And what course?"

"Worcester, maybe. To do Law."

"That's the college Abby wants to go to, too."

Jazz frowned. Sulvinder broke in.

"I'm not sure I want him to go to Oxford. I don't think that I'm clever enough to get in there myself."

"Nonsense," Jazz said, a smile returning to his face. "Of course you are."

Then he looked at his watch.

"We'd better be going in a minute," Jazz said. "I don't want to run into your father." He made a face at Lorna.

"Couldn't you get around Sulvinder's parents somehow?" Lorna asked.

Jazz shrugged.

"It's not so easy. Sikh girls aren't allowed to have boyfriends, full stop. Sometimes, these days, romance is condoned, but only if the couple plan to get married. But we're too young for that. If Sulvinder's parents were to accept a suitor, he would have to be more mature – more responsible, as they see it. Also, my father's white, so even though I don't look white and I'm a practising Sikh, they probably think that I have completely western values. It doesn't matter that I celebrate Diwali and Bhaisakhi, they wouldn't like my celebrating Christmas and Easter too."

Lorna knew the Kaurs, and thought that Jazz was being pessimistic, but didn't say so.

"Can I have a word with you alone before we go?" Joe asked. Sulvinder motioned Jazz to join her in the hallway. They needed time alone too, Lorna thought. But she wasn't sure that she wanted to be alone with Joe. He had hardly said a word since he arrived. He had been waiting for this moment. But his silence worried Lorna. It reaffirmed all the things he had said before about being intimidated by her more intelligent friends.

"How about Saturday night?" he said. "We could go to the Palais."

"We're not old enough to get in."

Joe smiled.

"I can get in anywhere these days. And you seem to have grown over the summer – all over."

Lorna smiled. It was true. She was three inches taller than she had been when she first started going out with Joe.

"Or, if you prefer, we could go to the pictures. I looked in the paper. There's one of those foreign films you're so fond of on at the Showcase."

"Really?"

Lorna hesitated. Joe had done her a favour tonight, though it was really for Sulvinder. But did that mean that she had to go out with him again, as a reward? She had promised herself that she would meet lots of new people this term. But the two boys who had asked her out so far were both ones who she knew already. Still, it was only the first day of term.

"I'll tell you what," she said. "I won't go out for a date with you on your own, but if you can get a group together to do something – dancing, whatever – I'll come along. How does that sound?"

Joe looked disappointed.

"I suppose it's a start," he said.

He walked over towards Lorna, so that they were standing close. She could feel his breath on her skin. She could smell him. He was so good looking, she thought. Maybe Joe was shallow compared to some people, but so what? Boys went out with girls for their looks all the time.

"Well, I'd better be going," Joe said, at last, regretfully.

"Yes," Lorna said. "You'd better."

From the hall, Jazz called.

"Joe? It's time."

Joe leant forward. He was going to try and kiss her, Lorna could tell. For a tantalizing moment, she thought that she was going to let him.

"'Bye."

She stepped to the side and he had no choice but to leave the room.

Lorna sat down on her bed with a sigh. When Sulvinder joined her a few moments later, she found Lorna crying.

"What did he say? Did he upset you?"

Lorna shook her head.

"No, it's just . . . I don't know what I'm doing any more. My head says I should tell him to get lost and my heart wants to hold him tight. And I end up doing neither and I'm feeling totally confused."

She told Sulvinder about what she'd agreed with Joe.

"Maybe you'd like to come out with us?" she suggested.

Sulvinder shook her head.

"I think that Jazz and I had better cool it for the moment. We've been seeing a lot of each other. I don't know. All the deception makes me uncomfortable. Whenever I say anything about him to my parents, they're really down on him and his family. If they knew how much I'd been keeping from them, they'd probably throw me out."

"Oh, come on," Lorna said. "It can't be as bad as all that. You said that people were becoming more tolerant these days."

"They are," Sulvinder said, "but it's slow. And what's tolerated for boys isn't always so easily allowed for girls."

The doorbell rang.

"Here he is," Sulvinder said. "My warder coming to double-check on me."

She went home.

172

Chapter 22

On Friday night, Lorna went to the pictures with Brian. It was a pleasant evening. The film was funny and sexy and very irreverent. She and Brian laughed a lot. Afterwards, they had a drink and he walked her home. Nothing was said. They were just being friends, that was all. As she stood at her doorstep, Lorna decided that, to be on the safe side, she ought not to invite him in. She held out her hand to shake his goodnight. Brian ignored it, leaning forward to kiss her on the cheek.

"See you on Monday," he said.

"Yes," she smiled back. "I enjoyed tonight. Thanks."

Her evening with Joe wasn't such a success. True to his word, Joe had assembled a crowd of people from the college and they all went to the Hippo, a club in Coddington. But as soon as they arrived there, the rest of the crowd seemed to melt away.

Instead of meeting lots of new people, Lorna found herself on her own with Joe for most of the evening.

They danced. It was easier than talking. There were so many areas she felt she had to avoid. Lorna wished that they could just shrug the past off and start anew. But they couldn't. When they talked, the failures of the summer were like a barrier between them. On the dance floor, though, it was different. Joe seemed to come alive. He was fun to be with. When they played the slow songs, she seemed to melt into his arms almost as overwhelmingly as she had before.

Only it wasn't before, it was now. At half past eleven, Lorna asked Joe to order her a taxi. But he insisted that she walk back to his house and get one from there. Lorna didn't feel like it. Once they were alone together, it would be hard not to let herself get carried away. Maybe she was being stupid, she thought. Maybe she should concentrate on just enjoying herself, like most of the other girls around her. But she had been badly hurt once before. If she fell again, she might never recover.

However, Joe insisted and Lorna was tired, so she agreed to walk back with him to his parents' house.

"It'll be much easier to get a taxi from there," Joe said.

Maybe he was right. Lorna would insist on ordering a taxi as soon as they arrived. Joe, she knew, would have other ideas.

It was September and the summer had started

to fade. A pale moon shed some light between the thin, grey streaks of cloud. As they passed Jazz's house, Lorna saw a door open and close. The tall, thin frame of Sulvinder's boyfriend stood in the hall, saying goodbye to somebody. Then a BMW came out of the garage and the figure in the doorway got into the car. As the person leaving opened the passenger door, the lights inside the car came on. Lorna recognized the driver: it was Jazz's father, Bill Jones. She recognized the girl in the passenger seat too. She had her hair swept back and was wearing her favourite dress. It was Abby.

Joe noticed nothing. He was too busy trying to put his arm around Lorna at every opportunity. When they got in, he called the taxi, then tried to kiss her again.

"What *is* it with you?" Lorna asked, only half her mind on what she was saying to him. "Do you think we can just fall back into what we had before the holiday fiasco?"

"Why not?" Joe said, looking hurt. "I still feel the same."

"But we're not the same," Lorna told him. "We've moved on. You've been out with someone else and so have I."

This news shocked Joe so much that he was silent for a moment. Then his eyes flashed angrily.

"Brian Kane," he said.

"No, not Brian," Lorna said, realizing as she said it that this wasn't strictly true. She had been out with Brian last night. It had been a kind of first date, but she didn't think of it as "going out" with him.

"Who then?"

"If you must know, it was someone in America. It wasn't serious. I was still busy getting over you."

Joe looked relieved.

"We're right for each other," he said. "Don't you see? We have fun together."

"We do," Lorna agreed, "but we're also very different from each other. We don't really have any friends in common. We don't even like the same things."

"We like *some* of the same things," Joe said, with a wicked glint in his eye, "and, as for the rest, we complement each other. Life would be boring if we were both the same, if we had the same taste in everything."

But wasn't that what most people were looking for? Lorna wondered – a person who was just like them, but of the opposite sex? Someone who they could share things with, but fancied as well? She wondered if Jazz and Abby had that. They were well matched in many ways – good looking, bright, glamorous. She could see that Jazz could be exactly the kind of guy Abby had been waiting for. But Lorna had thought that he was serious about Sulvinder. He certainly seemed serious two nights before. She couldn't believe that Jazz was cheating on Sulvinder with Abby. How could Lorna tell her best friend what she had seen? How could she ever face Abby again?

"Lorna, are you listening to me?" Joe asked.

"Er . . ."

Happily, before she could reply, there was a

hooting outside. Lorna grabbed her coat and rushed off for her taxi, not even giving Joe the chance to give her a goodbye kiss on the cheek.

Chapter 23

The next few weeks were among the most awkward of Lorna's life. She talked to Sulvinder about Jazz, trying to make friendly hints that something might be amiss, but Sulvinder seemed blind to the prospect that Jazz might be seeing someone else. Lorna began to think that she could have made a mistake, that there might be an innocent explanation for what she had seen.

Talking to Abby was even more difficult. How did you accuse someone of betraying a friendship? Lorna knew how some of the girls at her old school would do it. They would go in with fists flying and tongues wagging. There would be an all-out row and death threats would be issued. Then, somehow, it would all be resolved. The boy would be blamed, though one of them would still go out with him, and the girls would be friends again.

But Lorna couldn't work that way. Besides, it wasn't really her business. It was Sulvinder's.

And Sulvinder didn't show any interest, even when Lorna said that she thought she had seen Abby leaving Jazz's house one night.

"It can't have been – probably a friend of Jazz's sister's. Anyway, what were you doing round there? Have you been seeing Joe again?"

"Sort of."

Eventually, Lorna asked Abby directly, too.

"Are you friendly with Jazz's sister?"

That seemed the safest way of framing the question.

"Pamelajit? I've met her a couple of times, but I wouldn't say we were friends. Why?"

Lorna shrugged.

"It was only – I was going by the Jones's house the other night and I could have sworn I saw you getting into Jazz's dad's car."

Abby went scarlet. She said nothing. Then she got up and walked away from the table.

After that confrontation, Abby seemed to be doing her best to avoid Lorna and Sulvinder. Lorna missed seeing her, but thought that it was for the best. Also, she had new friends to engage her interest. Other boys were beginning to ask her out. She went out with three different boys in the run-up to Christmas. Two were in the year above her at college. The other was Brian Kane. Nothing at all serious came of any of the dates, but Lorna had some fun. She found it easier to relax in company than she used to. Of the boys who took her out, Brian was the easiest to be with. He had lots of conversation and didn't try anything on.

One of the people Lorna turned down for a date

was Joe. She became used to his hangdog expression when she told him that she was busy.

"Why won't you go out with me?" he asked in an urgent, pleading, almost pathetic voice.

Lorna didn't have an answer. Sometimes she thought she was nearly over him, and didn't want to put herself through the pain of separation again. Other times, she believed that she ought to give Joe another chance to prove himself. Then she would either find out that she still loved him, or realize that she was really over him. But this option seemed too risky. She felt safer the way she was going on, having casual dates with boys she liked, but wasn't going to fall in love with.

Christmas came and went. Lorna saw Joe at the end-of-term parties and danced with him a few times, but that was all. She expected him to give up and find himself another Stacey or Tracey or whatever her name was. If he did, she was sure it would hurt. However, Lorna's opposition seemed to make Joe more determined. He sent her a single red rose at Christmas, together with a very soppy card. Lorna preferred the Matisse card he'd sent her on Valentine's Day.

Then, in the Spring term, Joe started coming to General Studies classes. These were only once a week, and weren't compulsory, but Joe attended regularly. The classes discussed all sorts of subjects, from proportional representation to philosophical issues. Joe was his old self — cracking jokes in the discussion sessions, teasing anyone who said anything pretentious.

"Some people would argue that soap operas today fulfil the same role as Shakespeare did in his day," the lecturer said.

"Yeah, and the same people are probably the ones who think that Shakespeare's plays were written by an infinite number of monkeys locked in a room with a typewriter," Joe retorted.

"Yes," said the lecturer, "that's an interesting assertion."

"Only it's obvious," Joe said. "They've got it the wrong way round. Shakespeare wrote his own plays. The monkeys wrote *Eldorado*."

Everyone laughed. Lorna remembered how Joe's quips used to annoy her in English lessons at her old school. Now, though, she enjoyed his ability to make light of issues. She used to think that he was showing off his inferiority complex, but now she didn't think of what he did as showing off – she thought of it as performing. Some people had to give a performance all the time. It was their nature. Others, like herself, preferred to observe and consider. They could only talk to one or two people at a time. That didn't make them better or worse than extroverts like Joe, only different.

Joe, naturally, used the General Studies classes as an opportunity to chat Lorna up.

"Will you never give in?" Lorna asked him, one Friday afternoon.

"Not unless you give me a definite, unequivocal, absolutely irrefutable 'no'," Joe told her.

Lorna had to smile.

"No," she said.

"Is that 'No, you won't go out with me' or 'No, you won't give me a definite no'?" Joe asked.

"I don't know," Lorna admitted.

"So how about tomorrow night?" Joe suggested.

Lorna shrugged. Brian had tried to persuade her to go to a concert with him, but she had cried off, not liking the same music as him.

"Please," Joe said.

"I really don't know," Lorna told him. "All the things you said before about why we were wrong for each other — don't they still hold true?"

"Can't we at least find out?" Joe pleaded. "I can't remember what I said that morning. I was half asleep. I was angry with you. I probably didn't mean half of what I told you."

Was this true? Lorna couldn't tell. In her room on her own, maybe she could think it through. But with Joe in front of her, using all his charms, it was more difficult.

"Listen," Joe went on:

> *But like a sickness did I loathe this food:*
> *But as in health, come to my natural taste,*
> *Now I do wish it, love it, long for it,*
> *And will for evermore be true to it."*

Lorna recognized the speech. They were the lines which Demetrius used in *A Midsummer-Night's Dream* after the magic herb had caused him to fall back in love with Helena.

"So you *did* learn some Shakespeare for the exam," Lorna teased him.

Joe shook his head.

"If I'd revised for the exam, I would have done

182

better," he said. "No. I learnt those lines last night, for you."

Lorna smiled. She was impressed.

"All right," she said, still somewhat reluctantly, "we'll give it another go. What do you want to do?"

Joe put on his puckish grin.

"The rest of the family's going to my gran's for the weekend," he said. "Why don't you just come round for the evening?"

"You win," Lorna told him.

Then she went off to her next class, wondering what she'd let herself in for.

Chapter 24

"So you're giving Joe another chance?" Ric asked, as he dropped Lorna off.

"He talked me into it," Lorna admitted.

"Seemed a nice enough lad," Ric commented.

Lorna thought Ric was being diplomatic.

"Go on . . ." Lorna told him. "You were going to say, 'He seemed a nice enough lad, but . . .'."

"No buts," Ric replied. "I thought you'd outgrown him, that's all. Who's that other boy who takes you to the pictures?"

"You mean Brian? That's not serious."

"No? I've noticed him at college, seen the way he acts around you. He looks serious enough to me."

He let her out of the car.

"What's the betting that your mother's ready to go out when I get back?"

"At least two to one against," Lorna replied. "What are you two doing tonight?"

"I'm taking her for a meal at the best French

restaurant in town. Then, over the brandies afterwards, I'm going to have another go at persuading her to let me make an honest woman of her. What do you reckon to my chances?"

"Not a lot," Lorna replied. "I don't think Mum wants to be made an honest woman."

Ric shrugged.

"You never know. Third time lucky. See you!"

Lorna stayed in the driveway, staring at the road after Ric had driven away, lost in thought. She was so busy thinking about her mum and Ric that she almost didn't notice the Mini, driving back towards town along the road outside Joe's house. She recognized the car. It was Abby's mum's. And Abby's mum was in it. She must have been dropping Abby off at Jazz's. But no . . . that was ridiculous, jumping to conclusions. She could have been visiting friends, anything . . .

Lorna walked up to the door, which Joe opened before she could ring the bell.

"You looked like you couldn't make up your mind whether to come in," Joe told her, with a smile.

Lorna looked at him. He had washed his hair, giving it a fresh, frizzed look. He wore clean blue jeans and a new purple sweater which suited him. He looked good enough to eat.

"I . . . I thought that I saw someone."

"Who?"

"Abby's mother."

"And what would be strange about that?"

"Nothing. Except . . ."

Joe shrugged petulantly.

"She was probably dropping Abby off at Jazz's."

Lorna's face fell.

"At Jazz's? Why do you say that?"

Joe didn't seem to understand the big deal.

"Because she's always round there, isn't she?"

"Always? What do you mean? How would you know?"

"It's only round the corner, isn't it? I've seen her round here quite a few times over the last couple of months – arriving in the evening, leaving at night. Walking round in the day, too."

"You mean with Jazz?"

Lorna couldn't believe it. There was Sulvinder, stuck at home most weekends, pretending not to have a boyfriend, while all the time Jazz was seeing Abby.

"Sometimes with Jazz. I've seen her with his sister, Pam, and with their father, too – she seems to have become a regular member of the family recently. What's the problem?"

Lorna frowned.

"The problem is that he's still meant to be going out with Sulvinder."

Now it was Joe's turn to be shocked.

"You're kidding! I thought him and Sulvinder split up just after I saw you last. Sulvinder's parents were really down on Jazz."

"It looks like they were right to be," Lorna replied.

The news about Jazz put a damper on the evening. Lorna and Joe didn't get very romantic. They ended the evening curled up on a sofa together, watching videos. At one, Lorna caught a taxi home. When she got in, she was surprised to find that Mum was still up, though she was in her dressing gown. Lorna had completely forgotten about Ric's proposal, she'd been so preoccupied with Sulvinder.

"I'm glad you're back," Mum said to Lorna. "I was beginning to think that you were going to stay out for the evening."

"You know I wouldn't do that without telling you first."

"I know, but I was beginning to have my doubts."

"Is Ric here?"

"No. I sent him home."

Lorna sensed trouble. Ric usually stayed over on Saturday nights.

"I stayed up because I wanted to talk to you. The thing is, I think I may have done a very foolish thing."

That must mean she'd chucked Ric. Lorna's heart sank. That had to be it. Ric had got too serious and Mum had given him the push. It wouldn't be the first time she'd done that to a boyfriend.

"You do like Ric, don't you?" Mum asked.

"You know I do."

"Sometimes you're quite critical of him."

"So are you."

Mum sighed.

"Yes, I know. He's not perfect. But he *is* terribly sweet. The thing is – tonight he asked me to marry him."

"He said he would."

Mum looked surprised.

"He told you? The pig!"

"He told me about the other times too."

Mum raised her eyebrows.

"Then you probably realize that I couldn't just turn him down flat this time – not if I want to keep him."

Lorna weighed her mum's words.

"'Want to keep him' – Mum, you didn't say 'yes', did you?"

Mum gave Lorna a dubious look.

"Of course not. You know what I think about marriage. But I did say that – if you and Ben agreed – we'd buy a bigger house together and he could move in with us. What do you think?"

Lorna looked at her mother. She could see that she really wanted Lorna's opinion. It was a weird feeling, your own mother wanting your approval. Maybe Lorna would have fibbed if she'd had to. But it wasn't necessary.

"I think it's a great idea, Mum. I'm sure that Ben will, too."

"Oh, Lorna!"

Her mother gave her a great big hug.

"Thanks, love. You'll help me to persuade Ben, won't you, if he isn't sure?"

"Course I will. He likes Ric. It'll be fine."

"I hope so," Mum said. "It's a big step. But I hope so."

Lorna slept badly that night. There were so many things to think about. Her relationship with Joe was the least of them. There was Ric and her mum. In the next bedroom, she could hear Mum walking about, tossing and turning. She was having trouble sleeping, too. Things would change once they were living with Ric. But maybe it was time for a change.

Then there was Sulvinder, Jazz and Abby. Lorna had to do something about that. But what? She could call on Abby and tell her to stop seeing Jazz. But what good would that do? It might actually cause Jazz to split up with Sulvinder formally. Lorna could confront Jazz, tell him what she knew and try to persuade him to break off with Abby. But doing that might have the opposite effect. Or she could try telling Sulvinder again. Her friend could hardly insist that there was an innocent explanation this time.

Tell Sulvinder. That was what she had to do.

Chapter 25

"So we could have a bigger house, in Coddington maybe?"

"Maybe. Somewhere that's convenient for both Ric and me to get to work."

"Brilliant!"

"How do you feel about living with Ric, though?"

Ben shrugged.

"He practically lives here already, doesn't he?"

Mum smiled at Lorna in relief.

"It looks like the decision is made. I'd better ring Ric."

She paused.

"Where are you going?"

"I need to see Sulvinder."

"This early?"

Lorna muttered something about homework, then pulled her coat on and went out of the front door. Only as she was walking off into the rain did she remember that she and Sulvinder no longer did any of the same subjects. There was no possible reason for the two of them to get together over homework any more. Lorna had never been very good at making up stories.

Sulvinder's mum seemed pleased to see Lorna.

"To what do we owe this honour?"

"I just felt like coming round."

It took a cup of tea and two sticky sweets before Lorna was able to talk to Sulvinder alone, upstairs. Lorna's friend was in a cheerful mood. Lorna felt bad about having to bring her out of it.

"I had to come and see you," Lorna said, "though I feel really bad about the reason. It's Jazz."

She explained what Joe had told her the night before.

"I really want to think that there's an innocent explanation, but I don't see how there can be. From what Joe said, the less you've been seeing of Jazz, the more he's been seeing of Abby."

"I don't believe it," Sulvinder said.

"Do you mean you think Joe's lying?"

Slowly, Sulvinder shook her head. Tears were forming in her eyes.

"I mean, I can't believe it," Sulvinder said. "Not after all the things he . . . all the things . . ."

Then she collapsed in floods of tears. Lorna held her friend and passed her tissues until they were exhausted.

"What am I going to do?" Sulvinder asked, when she had recovered herself.

"Hadn't you better go and see him?" Lorna

asked. "You aren't going to give him up to Abby without a fight, are you?"

Sulvinder thought about it. Lorna knew that it was difficult for her. When people had disagreements, Sulvinder was always the conciliator, the person who smoothed things over. Confrontation wasn't in her nature.

"No," said Sulvinder. "I'm not going to give him up to Abby. I'll go there now."

She looked pleadingly at Lorna.

"Do you want me to come with you?" Lorna asked.

"Would you? At least as far as the door. I'm not sure I . . ."

The buses between Westtown and Coddington were useless on Sundays, so, despite the rain, they walked. Jazz's house was even farther from Sulvinder's than it was from Lorna's. Again and again, as they walked, Sulvinder rehearsed what she was going to say to Jazz. The rain got heavier. By the time the two girls arrived at the house, they were both soaked and bedraggled.

Sulvinder knocked on the door. It was answered by Bill Jones. The TV director was a smallish man in his early forties, with thinning fair hair.

"Is Jazz in?" she asked.

"No," Jazz's father said, awkwardly. "He's out."

Sulvinder's face fell still further.

"He's with her, isn't he?" she said. "Jazz is with Abby."

To Lorna's surprise, Bill Jones immediately nodded.

"Yes," the TV director said. "He is."

They stood on the doorstep staring at each other as the rain grew thicker.

"You'd better come in, Sulvinder," Bill Jones said. "I think you're owed an explanation."

Then he looked at Lorna.

"I'm sorry," he said. "I don't know you."

"Lorna."

"Lorna. Of course. Jazz and Abby – I mean, Jazz and Sulvinder have often talked about you. The thing is . . . this is family business. Would you mind if. . . ?"

"I'll go," Lorna said.

The director was apologetic.

"Please, it's raining. You could wait in . . ."

"No, really," Lorna said. "My boyfriend lives just round the corner. I'll go and see him. Will you be all right to get home, Sulvinder?"

"I'll run her home later," Bill Jones answered.

"OK. 'Bye!"

The door closed, leaving Sulvinder to whatever news Bill Jones had to tell her. Lorna put her head down and walked through the rain to Joe's.

Chapter 26

Lorna didn't realize until she got downstairs that today was Valentine's Day. This year, she had two cards waiting for her. One of them, she knew, would be from Joe. He had been pleased to see her yesterday morning. They had had lunch together. Lorna enjoyed it, though she quickly found herself running out of things to say.

Both of the Valentine's cards had printed addresses. Lorna couldn't tell for sure which one was from Joe. The first she opened was a soppy cartoon, and was signed by *"Guess Who"?* in green felt-tip. It could have been from any of a number of boys who had asked Lorna out over the last term-and-a-half.

Then she opened the second. It was a hand-painted card showing two silhouettes, embracing. It must have been really expensive. Inside, the message was printed in anonymous black ink.

"Don't make me wait any longer. Now could be our time." Beneath it was a simple black "x".

Joe was right, Lorna supposed. She had made him wait long enough. Why was she making such a big deal over going out with him again? Hadn't she told Jazz's father on Sunday that Joe was her boyfriend? She must tell Joe her decision soon.

But Lorna had something else on her mind. She hadn't heard from Sulvinder since leaving her at Jazz's house on Sunday. Lorna guessed that she hadn't had the opportunity to make a call in private. Yet she was anxious to know what had happened. Suppose she met Abby before seeing Sulvinder? How should she treat her?

In the event, this was exactly what happened. Lorna didn't see Sulvinder around in the morning break, and she had Art for the second part of the morning. Abby was there, working on her collage depicting the fashion industry. She nodded at Lorna and gave her a friendly smile. Lorna nodded coolly back, then went to work on her own collage, a complicated picture of the planet Earth, seen from space.

Towards the end of the class, Abby wandered over to Lorna.

"Did you hear about Jazz's party on Saturday?" she asked. Lorna was astonished. She had never expected Abby to bring up Jazz's name herself.

"Jazz is having a party?" she mumbled.

"Yes. Like the one he had last year. You can't have forgotten. His eighteenth. The one where you got off with Joe."

"No," Lorna admitted. "I haven't forgotten."

"So the question is," Abby went on, "who are you going to go with? I'm curious."

Lorna had had enough.

"No," she said. "The question is how you have the effrontery to start going on about Jazz and his party after you've been seeing him secretly for over three months. I've known you for years and years and I'd never have believed that you were capable of acting the way you are! You disgust me!"

Abby looked shocked. For once, she was at a loss for words. Lorna put her things away. As she did this, Abby started to speak.

"I don't know what you think you know," Abby said slowly, "but it sounds like you've got it wrong. There's an explanation."

"All right," said Lorna, "go on then. Convince me. It had better be a pretty amazing explanation."

"I can't," Abby admitted. "What I mean is, there are other people I'd have to talk to first. Jazz, for one . . ."

"You mean, so that you can get your stories straight?" Lorna asked. "Forget it, Abby. Save your explanations for Sulvinder. She's the one being hurt by all of this, not me."

Before Abby could reply, Lorna stormed off.

Lorna looked around for Sulvinder all lunch time, but her friend wasn't there. It wasn't until the evening that Sulvinder showed up at Lorna's house.

"What did you say?" Lorna asked, once they were alone.

"I told him what you'd told me," Sulvinder said.

"Did he deny it?" Lorna asked.

"Not exactly."

"He admitted that he'd been seeing Abby?"

"Yes, but . . ."

Sulvinder looked uncomfortable.

"What do you mean, 'but'? You're not still going out with him, are you?"

Sulvinder smiled sheepishly.

"Yes, I am."

"So he's said that he won't see Abby any more?"

"Not exactly."

Lorna couldn't believe her ears.

"I don't understand."

Sulvinder spoke slowly.

"There are some things I can't explain, not yet."

"Why not?"

"Because other people are involved. There are secrets. You know how it is."

"But I don't."

"I wish I could tell you, but . . . believe me, it's not what you think."

"Have you spoken to Abby?"

"Not yet. But I think that Jazz is going to talk to her tonight."

"Is he going to finish with her?"

Sulvinder stood up.

"I'm sorry, Lorna. I don't mean to be mysterious. Look, Jazz is having a party on Saturday."

"I know. Abby invited me."

This seemed to surprise Sulvinder.

"You and Joe are invited to the party," she said. "Hopefully, Jazz, Abby and I ought to be able to explain things there. I'm afraid that it will have

to wait until then. Now I'd better go. I don't like
keeping secrets from you. I'm sorry."

"It's OK. When it comes down to it, this is your
business, not mine."

"You're right," Sulvinder said. "It is."

When she'd gone, Lorna rang Joe and told him
about the party.

"Weird," he said. "What do you think's going
on?"

"I've no idea," Lorna told him. "Oh, and thanks
for the card. It's lovely."

"You're welcome. Thanks for mine."

The next day, in Lorna's Communication Studies
class, Brian Kane asked her if she was going to
Jazz's party on Saturday.

"I think so," she said.

"Can I take you?"

"Er . . ."

Brian started to backtrack.

"I mean, I could give you a lift."

"Thanks. That's nice of you, but . . . I've sort of
started going out with Joe again. I'll be going
round to his house beforehand."

"Oh."

"Sorry," Lorna repeated. "It's not that I . . ."

She didn't know what she meant to say.

"It's OK," Brian said, trying to recover some
dignity. "Just wanted to make sure that you had
someone to go with."

In Art, Abby walked over to Lorna.

"You know, I didn't know what you were going

on about yesterday. Now I do, though."

"Do you?"

Lorna wanted to get up and walk away, but the lesson had only just started.

"I'm surprised at you, Lorna," Abby said. "How could you think that I'd do something like that to Sulvinder?"

"What else is there to think?"

"Sometimes," Abby told her, "life's more complicated than even you imagine, Lorna Haines."

Then she went back to her collage. Lorna didn't have a proper conversation with either her or Sulvinder for the rest of the week. She had no idea what on earth was going on.

Chapter 27

"Maybe we should just stay here," Lorna said to Joe, as they got ready to go to the party.

"Fine by me," Joe said. "Then I'll have the best-looking girl at the party all to myself."

He began to play with the back of Lorna's dress. She shook herself free. There had been a time, she realized, when a touch like that would have sent shivers of anticipation down her spine. Had the spark gone from her relationship with Joe? Or was it just the unsettled mood she was in which was stopping anything from happening?

"No," Lorna said after a pause. "I think we must go to this party. Like I told you, I want to know what's going on."

"If we arrive together, it'll be official, you know," Joe said. "Everyone will know that you're going out with me again."

"Or, to put it another way, that you're going out with me."

"If you say so."

"People can call it what they like," Lorna said. "At the moment, I'm not willing to make any commitments beyond one evening at a time. If you can't settle for that, then tough."

Joe frowned.

"I was hoping . . ."

"I'm sorry, Joe. This is a weird time."

He smiled grudgingly.

"OK, I guess. But how about a kiss to be going on with?"

Lorna kissed him. It was a long, hard kiss, which left his lips tainted with lipstick. Joe got a tissue and wiped them.

"That tastes strong," he said.

"It wasn't the lipstick that tasted strong," Lorna muttered. "It was the woman wearing it." She spoke up. "Come on. Let's go."

The party was in full swing when they arrived. It was a shock to Lorna, seeing so many people from her old school. She said hello to Melissa.

"Have you seen Sulvinder?"

"She's downstairs, dancing with Jazz."

"Oh."

Lorna guessed that that was good. Joe went off to deposit their coats and get the drinks. Lorna looked around.

"Have you seen Abby?" she asked Melissa.

"Hardly. Not since the summer."

"Oh. Right."

Melissa drifted off. Her friendship with Abby had lasted less than a year. Maybe Lorna ought to feel glad that it had taken her nearly twelve years to stop being Abby's friend. Maybe it was some kind of a record.

Joe came back with the drinks.

"White wine spritzer, right?"

"What else?"

They drank. Lorna remembered the excitement of the same party at this time last year. She remembered how, with every drink, Joe had got better looking. Or maybe it wasn't the drink, maybe it was that she'd taken off her glasses. Tonight, with her artificial twenty/twenty vision, he didn't look bad. Better than average, certainly. A little vain, perhaps. She had noticed the way he checked himself out in passing mirrors.

They were still standing in the hall. As the front door opened and someone else arrived, Lorna saw a familiar car pulling up in the driveway. Brian had taken her out to the Showcase in it the day after he passed his driving test. She remembered how she'd snubbed him when he asked if he could take her to this party. She stood watching the door in silence, regretting her hasty decision. Joe watched too. She and he really had nothing to say to each other any more. All they had was a fading physical attraction.

Then the door opened again and Lorna felt as if she'd been kicked in the stomach. Brian hadn't come to the party alone. Accompanying him, in a tight, surprisingly low-cut red dress was her former friend, Abby.

But to Lorna's eyes, it wasn't Abby who looked sensational tonight. It was Brian. He had had his hair cut back and wore tinted, half-moon glasses which suited him really well. Somehow, his face no longer seemed so thin. He looked more . . . intellectual. Also, Brian reminded her of someone — the boy called Michael she had had the brief romance with in America. Or maybe it was that Michael had reminded her of Brian. Maybe that was what had drawn Lorna to the American boy in the first place.

Coolly, Abby said hello to Lorna and Joe. Joe replied, but Lorna said nothing. She shot a reproachful glance at Brian then hurried upstairs, where she hid herself in the toilet for fifteen minutes. She didn't cry. She sat on the closed lid, thinking. Then someone knocked on the door. Lorna flushed the toilet, splashed her face, and came out. She knew what she had to do.

"Lorna! You've been ages!"

"I had some thinking to do."

Joe looked blank.

"Oh. OK. Want to dance?"

"No," Lorna said. "That's all we ever seem to do well together, dance. I want to talk. But first, perhaps you could get me another drink, please?"

"Sure."

Joe went off. Lorna stood in the hallway, watching people arrive, taking deep breaths. Then Sulvinder came up from the dancing in the cellar.

"Lorna! There you are. Look, Jazz and I want to talk to you, to explain everything. Could we go up to his room?"

"In a few minutes," Lorna said. "There's something that I've got to sort out with Joe first."

"All right," Sulvinder said. "We'll see you up there."

There was a crush in the kitchen. Joe must be having trouble getting the drinks. As she stood in the hall, Brian wandered out, on his own.

"Lorna," he said. "You look lovely tonight."

"Thank you," said Lorna. "So do you."

Brian blushed and Lorna realized what she had said.

"Sorry," she said, "I was a million miles away. I suppose I should have said 'so does Abby' or something like that."

"I think," said Brian, "that I preferred your original statement."

He walked away. Lorna cursed herself. Why had it taken her until tonight to realize how much she liked Brian, with his lanky good looks and his wry sense of humour? Why did it take him going out with Abby to make her realize that she'd been taking his company for granted?

"Your drink, ma'am."

"Thanks," Lorna said to Joe. "Let's find somewhere quiet to talk."

They went to the conservatory, which was off the back of the living room, where Lorna thought they wouldn't be disturbed. She couldn't find the light switch, but it didn't matter. The moon was shining brightly in a clear, dark blue sky. Joe looked very handsome in the ethereal light.

"What did you want to tell me?" he asked.

"That it's over," Lorna said. "I'm sorry, but I'm not in love with you any more."

Joe blinked.

"I thought . . ."

"I know what you thought. But I think we've been kidding ourselves. It ended last summer. And you were right. We're too different from each other. And it isn't just that. The spark we had before. It's gone. You must realize that."

Joe nodded slowly.

"I thought if we gave it time . . ."

"We've already given it long enough," Lorna said softly. "It's time to move on. I know you've been trying hard. That lovely Valentine card you sent me . . ."

"It was nothing special," Joe mumbled. "A silly cartoon."

Lorna didn't take in what he was saying. She was too busy completing the speech she'd prepared.

"I'd rather we finished tonight," she said, "with no bad feelings, than go on, slowly falling apart. What we had last year was special. I'll never forget it."

"Me neither," Joe said.

He was crying. Lorna took a tissue from her pocket and wiped the tears from his face. Then she kissed him softly on the cheek.

"I've got to go," she said. "Will you be all right?"

Joe nodded. Lorna hurried out of the conservatory. She had to move quickly, into the light, otherwise she would start crying herself.

Lorna climbed the stairs, oblivious to the party around her. She wanted to be alone. As she reached the landing, a door opened. Jazz's face peered out.

"Lorna!" he said. "We were wondering what had happened to you."

He ushered her into his bedroom. It was a big room, but Lorna didn't take in the decor. She found herself staring at the two girls sitting on the bed. Each looked beautiful in her own way. Both were smiling: Abby nervously, Sulvinder contentedly. Lorna sat where Jazz pointed her to, an armchair in the corner of the room.

"I think you're owed an explanation," he said, sitting between the two girls. "You told Sulvinder about me seeing Abby. I don't blame you. Really, I should have told her myself. But the situation was a delicate one for Abby and my family. We weren't ready. In a sense, you forced our hand."

"I'm sorry," Lorna said. "I've still got no idea what you're talking about."

"I'm sorry, too," Abby said. "When you had a go at me on Monday, I had no idea what you knew, or how. It's taken me a long time to get my feelings sorted out. If Jazz had had his way, he'd have told Sulvinder much sooner. But, for now, we've decided to just tell a few close friends, starting with you two."

Lorna looked at Sulvinder in amazement. How could she sit there so placidly when Jazz and Abby seemed to be declaring their love for each other?

"The thing is," Jazz said, pausing to take a breath before he finished the sentence, "Abby is my sister."

Lorna looked from one to the other, trying to comprehend the nature of the joke.

"Half-sister, really," Abby continued, nervously. "My mum acted in a TV play that Bill Jones directed the year Jazz was born. They had an affair. This was before she got religion – it was all very tacky. Mum hoped Bill would leave Jazz's mum, but he didn't. Mum never told me who my father was. She refused to have anything further to do with him. Then, last year, Jazz's family moved to Coddington. Part of the reason for their coming to the area was that Bill, my father, wanted to get in touch with my mum and try and get to know me. But Mum refused to talk to him. Then Sulvinder invited me to Jazz's party. I told Mum where I was going and she blew up. She told me I couldn't go to the party.

"But you know me. The more she said I couldn't go, the more determined I was to turn up. When I found out who Jazz's father was, I began to work out the truth. I knew that my mother had worked for Bill Jones, and I'd noticed that she changed the subject a couple of times when his name came up. Now I realized that he might be my father.

"It was weird, meeting Jazz and Pamelajit and guessing that I was their sister, but they didn't know it. I couldn't handle it for long and left early. I was a bit freaked out for a while after that. My mum and I were hardly talking – she finally admitted that Bill Jones was my father, but wouldn't let me have anything to do with him or Jazz and Pamelajit. I got depressed and took it out on everyone. I even remember having a row with you about your going out with Joe."

Jazz continued the story.

"Sulvinder would often mention Abby when she was round here, and my dad used to ask questions about her. When he heard that I was going to Abby's birthday party, he told me the full story. The party was weird. Both Abby and I knew who the other was, but neither of us knew whether the other knew. After it, my dad contacted Abby's mother again. Eventually, she agreed that Abby could come and meet my father, Pamelajit and me, if she wanted to.

"So, for the last few months, Abby's been coming round here regularly and we've been getting to know each other, as a family. But we didn't want people to know. My father behaved very badly. It all happened a long time ago, but it's still painful to both our mothers. Also, it would hurt my mother a great deal if the local Sikh community found out about it."

Lorna felt herself overwhelmed.

"You were right, Abby," she said. "Sometimes life is even more complicated than a Victorian novel. I'm so sorry I doubted you . . . both of you."

"It's not your fault," Abby said. "I would probably have jumped to the same conclusion. You and Sulvinder are my best friends. I should have told you what was going on. Instead I let myself get distanced from you."

Lorna shook her head in amazement.

"All that time I thought you were after Jazz," she said. "And really the one you wanted was Brian."

"Brian!" Abby said. "Surely you don't think he's my type?"

"You came with him tonight."

"I came with him because he asked me. I needed a lift."

Lorna wasn't convinced.

"But lots of other boys must have wanted to bring you."

Abby shrugged.

"They may have wanted to, but they didn't ask. I don't get asked out very often and it's always by the wrong lads. Most of them think I'm too stuck up and haughty."

Jazz laughed. Abby punched him in the thigh, the way a sister might do.

"I can't help it!" she said. "It's just the way I am. Anyway, Lorna, Brian Kane isn't in the least interested in me. He spent the whole journey asking me whether he'd got any chance whatsoever of prising you away from Joe."

"He did?"

"I really don't understand what you see in Joe. He might be good looking, but Brian's a whole lot nicer."

"You know something?" Lorna said. "I think you're right."

Sulvinder and Jazz were smiling.

"Come on," Abby said. "Let's leave these two lovebirds alone for a while."

They went out onto the landing. Abby spoke in a hushed tone.

"Sulvinder's decided to tell her parents about her and Jazz tomorrow. They need all the time they can get alone together tonight, in case her parents ban her from seeing him again."

"Do you think that'll happen?" Lorna asked.

"I don't know," Abby replied. "But if they love each other as much as they seem to, they'll find a way to convince them in the end."

"I hope so," Lorna said. "They deserve to."

Abby smiled. She was more relaxed than Lorna had ever seen her before.

"There he is," Abby said. "Good luck!"

Brian raised his glass to Lorna as she walked over to him. He was standing in the living room on his own.

"I'd ask you to dance," he said, "but you already know how bad I am at it."

"It's OK," Lorna said. "I've done enough dancing recently to last me quite a while."

"I saw Joe leaving earlier. Did you have a row?"

"Not exactly," Lorna told him. "More a parting of the ways."

Brian's eyes lit up.

"Anyway," she said, "what happened to your date? You seem to have deserted her."

Brian gave an awkward grin.

"Abby's really great," he said. "But . . ."

"But I thought you didn't like her!" Lorna interrupted. "I seem to remember you at the college freshers' evening, going on about how she looked like a plastic doll."

Brian squirmed a little.

"If I said that, I was exaggerating. But anyway, I only criticized her looks," Brian said. "I didn't criticize her as a person. I like Abby, though I don't fancy her. She's become a nicer person since she moved to the college. But that's not why I asked her out."

"Why *did* you ask her out?" Lorna said.

"Because I thought it might make you jealous. Because I'm fed up with playing Mr Nice Guy, waiting for you to realize how I felt about you. I sent you a Valentine two years running and what did you do straight after each one? You started going out with Joe Green! He's not good enough for you. Maybe I'm not either, but I think I deserve a chance to prove myself. Don't you?"

Lorna nodded.

"You!" she said. "I only worked it out as I walked over to you just now. You sent me both of those lovely cards."

Brian smiled as he leant down and took her in his arms. Lorna let him hold her close. It felt right. Everything had nearly gone so wrong, but it seemed to be coming right in the end.

"Will you be my girlfriend?" Brian asked quietly.

"Of course I will," Lorna whispered back, pressing her body more tightly against his. "You're a very patient boy, Brian Kane. And I've been a very stupid girl."

Before replying, Brian leant down so that their lips were nearly meeting. His voice was gentle, full of warmth, and humour, and love.

"Kiss me, stupid!"

And she did.

Coming soon from Point Romance.

A Winter Love Story
Jane Claypool Miner

Jessica was pleased and surprised how quickly the time went. She and Davey sang for about an hour and they discovered that they both had a fondness for old songs. He had a very low, pleasant baritone voice and her contralto blended well. She didn't have as big a voice as he did, but that didn't seem to matter to him. "It's not the Metropolitan Opera," he said. "You'll do fine."

When she insisted she had to leave, he said, "You know, you're quite good."

She shook her head and said, "No, not good enough. I had my voice checked out when I was about fourteen. We went to two singing teachers, and they both agreed that I had a pleasant voice. The kind of voice that ends up singing in churches."

"You're probably more interested in something else, anyway, aren't you?" Davey asked.

"Yes, as a matter of fact, I'm interested in quite a few other things," Jessica answered. "I'm interested in mathematics and literature, and I think I might want to be a writer."

"A songwriter?"

"Could be," Jessica admitted. "Once in a while I work out some songs on my guitar."

"I'd like to hear some of them," Davey said.

"Maybe you will," Jessica answered. "But tell

me about you. You have a good voice, and you're already singing professionally. How old are you?"

"I'm eighteen," Davey answered. "I finished high school last June and took a six-month trip to Europe with my mother. Now I'm waiting to get into college next fall. So I took this job up here for the winter season."

He had a very direct and simple way of speaking. No attempt to impress her and yet, Jessica could guess that he was a very, very rich boy.

Perhaps he'd read her mind because he said, "I'm one of those people who isn't quite sure *what* to do with the rest of his life. Money isn't a major consideration."

"You mean you're loaded," Jessica teased him.

He smiled and said, "I guess that's what you could call it. At any rate, I could get by without working for the rest of my life, but I *want* to work. The problem is, I can't decide if I want to work as a stockbroker or a musician."

"That's a funny choice," Jessica said. "When you sing, you seem as though you love it so much. It seems like it would be an easy decision for you."

"Music?" Davey sighed. "I suppose the typical plan would be to pursue a musical career – defy the stodgy family and all that. But my family is only half-stodgy. I'm in a position where I can't win."

"Or maybe you can't lose."

"Yes." He smiled quickly. Jessica noticed that he had a funny way of tilting his head slightly to one side when he talked about his family. Until now, she'd seen only a very straightforward, self-assured young man. Now she could see that he was still a boy – a boy who was anxious to please.

Davey seemed to want to talk about it. "The problem is, my mother is a failed singer. Well, I don't know if she really failed. I think what she really did was marry and give up her musical career. And so ever since I've been a little kid, she's been pushing me toward music. She actually managed to get me in a couple of movies when I was a kid. And I was on a TV series for a year until my dad put his foot down and sued for custody. He won."

"So now you live with your dad?"

"I go back and forth."

"Where is your father?" Jessica asked.

"He's in New York City. He expects me to go to Harvard and follow in his footsteps. My mother expects me to go to UCLA or USC while I break into show business. She got me this job."

"Yes, Angel told me," Jessica answered.

"What else did Angel say?" he asked.

"Not much." She stood up again.

Davey looked upset. "Angel and I have dated some, but it's nothing serious. Not to me, anyway."

"Is it to Angel?" Jessica asked.

Davey shrugged. "I don't know. Angel is . . . Angel."

"I really have to go now," Jessica said. "The girls will be waiting for me."

"But you will be there tonight?" Davey asked.

Jessica laughed. "You've asked me that three

times now. I always do what I say, Davey. Don't worry."

Davey smiled and Jessica felt like patting his cheek or giving him a hug. She didn't, though. She was in no position to be nice to a little lost stray, who might be another girl's boyfriend.

Point Romance

Look out for the new Point Romance
mini series coming soon:

First Comes Love

by Jennifer Baker

Can their happiness last?

When eighteen-year-old college junior Julie Miller
elopes with Matt Collins, a wayward and rebellious
biker, no one has high hopes for a happy ending.
They're penniless, cut off from their parents, homeless
and too young. But no one counts on the strength of
their love for one another and
commitment to their vows.

Four novels, *To Have and To Hold, For Better or
Worse, In Sickness and in Health,* and *Till Death Us Do
Part,* follow Matt and Julie through their first
year of marriage.

Once the honeymoon is over, they have to deal with the
realities of life. Money worries, tensions, jealousies,
illness, accidents, and the most heartbreaking decision
of their lives.
Can their love survive?

Four novels to touch your heart...

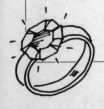